nude

Nuala Ní Chonchúir is an Irish short fiction writer and poet, born Dublin 1970. Her short fiction collections *The Wind Across the Grass* (2004) and *To the World of Men, Welcome* (2005) were published by Arlen House. Her poetry collections *Tattoo:Tatú* (2007) and *Molly's Daughter* (2003) appeared from the same publisher. She has won many literary prizes, including RTÉ Radio's Francis MacManus Award and the Cecil Day-Lewis Award. Nuala lives in Galway with her partner and children.

nuala
ní chonchúir

nude

SALT

LONDON

PUBLISHED BY SALT PUBLISHING
Fourth Floor 2 Tavistock Place, Bloomsbury, London WC1H 9RA United Kingdom

© Nuala Ní Chonchúir, 2009

First published 2009

Printed in Great Britain by the MPG Books Group,
Bodmin and King's Lynn

Typeset in Swift 11 / 14

ISBN 978 1 84471 642 5 paperback

Salt Publishing Ltd gratefully acknowledges
the financial assistance of Arts Council England

1 3 5 7 9 8 6 4 2

For Finbar,
for everything

CONTENTS

'Nudity is a form of dress.'
—John Berger, *Ways of Seeing*

MADONNA IRLANDA

THE GUIDE BOOK said not to smile at men, that it is not a part of the culture and might be misinterpreted as flirting. For the first few days I swallowed my thanks for directions and nodded sternly at both men and women. But the people were nice, so I soon gave that up and said '*Merci*' —with smiles—to all. I got lost a lot at first, though Paris is not a confusing city. Victor, my ex-husband, used to say I couldn't find my way out of a paper bag. *Ex*-husband. That always sounds like I'm trying to state a position, make myself known; when I say it in conversation, I hear my own defensiveness.

Victor was always pass-remarkable. He could never help pointing out where I was going wrong with a painting, or with my friendships, or with the way I boiled an egg. He often told me he was jealous of me, as if that was my fault, and it was OK for him to feel like that. When we were writhing through the last throes of pretending we had a future, he told me that for the first years of our marriage, I was crap in bed. And after that I was 'only passable'.

'Virgins are notoriously crap in bed, Victor,' I said.

'But I was good, Magda.' He wore a horribly vain crease to his mouth when he said that.

But, Victor gave me the surname Bolding which, added to Magdalone—my mother's skewed-up version of a Bible name—always felt more 'me' than Magda Foley. I'm grateful for that.

Does it matter, really, how love starts or why it goes on?

Together, Victor and I were easy and nothingish, unastonishing. We fuddled through twelve years who-knows-how. I had decided I loved him the first time I met him, drinking whiskey in The Long Hall in Dublin. He was the opposite of the men I'd loved before. Victor had money and interminable anecdotes about the shop floor in Clery's where he worked, but I liked his ursine face—he was snouty and pug-eyed—and the streak that made him wear a suit when everyone else wore denim. I mistook him for an eccentric, I think, and he was attracted by what he called my 'arty fartyness'. We stayed together too long and became husks of ourselves. After we separated—and when I shook off the guilt and sadness—I went to Paris. That was my first time. I was glad Victor and I hadn't been there together—at least it wouldn't be sodden with memories of us, as Italy was.

Every tourist site we went to as a couple, each street and café, holds our ghosts; they spectre around me when I revisit, and I'm reminded of happiness we once had. Victor and I did have good times. But I suspect we never loved each other. Not properly. And I never had any idea that he thought I was useless in bed.

I had come to Paris in search of dead artists and living ones. My will to paint had evaporated and I wanted the city to give me the jizz-up that eluded me in Dublin; I expected a lot but was willing to accept Paris's gifts slowly. My first few days, I crawled the streets of Montparnasse, fingering paint tubes in dim art shops and eating custard-heavy pastries from sugar-smelling *patisseries*. I sat on a bench in the Luxembourg Gardens, sucking in the freshness, and watching the ambling tourists and young parents with pram-bound babies. Day by day I started to feel it was all right for me to be there among them.

The hotel I had found sat on a narrow street, chock-a-block with furriers—one had the tragically funny name 'Foxy-Minky'. My room was a slice of a bigger one that had been carved up; its mushroom-hued walls made me nauseous, but it had a soft, blue carpet and double windows onto my own balcony. At night, with the wall lamp on, and all of Paris still busy outside, the room was cosy.

Victor had instructed me to visit an old boarding school dorm mate of his—an artist.

'Drop in on Mike Farrell,' he had said, 'you'll like him.'

'But will he like me?'

'Everyone likes you, Magda,' Victor said.

I was surprised by his sincerity and sudden tears dropped down my cheeks. These were the kind of tears I thought were as dead as my marriage, but clearly the well still burbled.

'Sorry,' I said, swiping at my cheeks with a tissue.

'Your bladder was always too near to your eye.' Victor hugged me. 'Enjoy yourself in Paris. Go and see Farrell and tell him he still owes me a wad. The fucker.'

I sat on my hotel bed and looked at the man's address in my diary; I was sick at the idea of turning up at his door, but also felt I would be letting Victor down if I didn't. For all I knew Farrell was expecting me. I scribbled a note on my hotel's headed paper, planning to shove it in his letter box and scarper.

The morning air smelt cool; water runnelled down street-sides and shopkeepers swept their paths. I walked down avenue de Maine and easily found the beehive shape of La Ruche—the colony on Passage Dantzig where Farrell and his family lived. The building lay in a gated garden, its turquoise front door flanked by busty caryatids. In the hall-way there was a wall of postboxes and, as I stuffed my note in the one with Farrell's name, a man came down the stairs. He stopped to look at me and lit a smoke. I rushed through the garden to the street and the man tipped out behind me. He walked close to me on the footpath—I could smell his cigarette—so I went into a haberdasher's and stood in front of a rack of ribbons. I could sense the man at the window; I turned away, picked up a roll of black ribbon and ran its sheen through my fingers.

'If it's for your hair, I'd get a red one.' He was in the doorway. I turned to tell him to leave me alone and only then registered his Irish accent; he walked in. 'Here.' He took the spool of black from my hand and replaced it with a red.

'Micheal?'

'That's me.'

I blushed and dropped the ribbon and it unwound itself like a miniature red carpet across the floor. Micheal ran after it, whooped, and grabbed it. He took a scissors from the counter, cut the ribbon to the spot where it had unravelled, and paid for it. The haberdasher looked bemused and I grinned at her, before taking the coil of ribbon that Micheal was holding in front of my nose.

'Thank you,' I said.

'Victor told me you were as clumsy as all-get-out.' He held the shop door open for me.

Micheal brought me to Les Deux Magots; I'd passed it on my wanderings but, intimidated by the swirling efficiency of the waiters, I hadn't gone in.

'This was Wilde's local,' Micheal said, after ordering a jug of hot chocolate for us to share and a brandy for himself. 'And Picasso first met Dora Maar here.'

'Really?' I said. 'Who else?'

'Hemingway was a regular. De Beauvoir and Sartre.' Micheal lit a cigarette. 'Farrell, of course.' He blew smoke at me. 'Are you a Brit?'

'No.'

'You talk like one.' He stirred his brandy into the chocolate. 'What are you doing here?'

'I want . . . *need* to start painting again.'

'Fair enough. I suppose you'd like to see inside The Hive?' I nodded and he stood up.

'Right now?' I asked. 'I'm sure your wife wouldn't want a visitor this early in the day.'

'Her Maj is gone to London with the kids.'

'For good?' The question fell from my mouth before I could stop it.

'To get away from me for a few weeks.' Micheal downed his drink and shuddered his lips. 'Art and marriage are a poor match, Magda. They suck the guts out of each other.' He crooked his elbow in mock chivalry. 'Shall we?'

I snuck into a working *atelier* on rue de la Grande Chaumière and stood at the back of a class in progress. The students were young; the boys and girls had those pretty-pinched French faces and a weary confidence. Their model was a black man; his penis hung dark and huge between his straddled thighs and his skin—the darkest I had ever seen—bulged over his bones. I watched him squat and bend at intervals, under the instruction of the teacher. I looked around the rest of the studio, at the dirty easels and piles of palettes. High on one wall, someone had put a gilt frame around the words 'Rilke loves Clara'. The teacher walked towards me, his arm questioningly out-stretched, and I ducked out of the room.

That evening, I coaxed Micheal out of his studio with wine.

'*Le Beaujolais Nouveau est arrivé!*' I said, holding up two bottles and parroting the banners that hung in all the bistros we drank in. '*Le Beaujolais Nouveau est arrivé!*'

'*Le Beaujo! C'est beau!*' he shouted back at me, getting glasses and a corkscrew; I sat down at the kitchen table.

'Hey, I went into an *atelier* today, part of an art school,' I told Micheal. 'They were doing life drawing. The model was beautiful.' I wiggled my glass at him. 'You know, I think Rilke might have gone there. Was he a painter as well as a poet?'

'Rilke was a sponging ponce.' He popped the wine cork.

'And who was Clara?'

'A sculptor—Rilke's wife, God help her.' He winked at me and laughed, acknowledging, I guessed, his own wife. He poured some wine for himself and eyed me. 'So, you want to pose for me, Mrs Bolding, is that what you're saying?'

'What makes you say that?'

'You're like every Irish man, woman and child—a slieveen, slyly sliding around things instead of saying them out.' His face looked grim.

'Fuck off, Micheal, and pour my wine.'

He laughed. 'You're a cheeky bitch, Magda,' he said, 'sitting at my table with your child's smile and foul tongue. But, sure, that's why I'm mad about you.' He poured, chinked his glass to mine, kissed my cheek and we drank. 'I'm starting a political thing that you could pose for, if you wanted.'

'Oh, yeah?'

'I'm calling it *Madonna Irlanda*. It's sort of classical: Ireland as a nude, with her arse cocked to the Brits, waiting to be fucked.' He puffed on his fag. 'In the typical Irish way.'

'Spoken like a true ex-pat. Ex-Paddy, I should say.' I

sipped the cool Beaujolais. 'I'll pose,' I said, 'but you're to keep your paws off me.'

Micheal held up his palms. 'With Farrell on the job, your virtue is secure.'

We went to the Louvre to see *L'Odalisque*, one of the Boucher portraits Micheal wanted to base his painting on. We stopped at the inevitable bistro on rue de Rivoli and Micheal had his two morning beers. Charged up, he marched me through the dim art gallery, bouncing up marble stairs and along corridors ahead of me, towards the Sully Wing.

'Ta-dah!' he said, when we reached the painting, as if he were responsible for it. The portrait showed the artist's wife, lying on her stomach on a lake of blue velvet, her behind exposed.

'Meaty, isn't she?' I said.

'Could you do up your hair like hers?' Micheal pushed his hands into my hair, frowning. 'Jesus, it's like kelp hanging around your face.'

'Get away from me.' I pulled his hands down and studied Boucher's portrait. 'I'm more concerned about the bare bum than the hairstyle.'

'Look how pink it is—he must've slapped the arse off her. Naughty, naughty, Madame Boucher.' Micheal laughed. 'The other painting is better, the one he did of Louisa O'Murphy, the Irish girl who was the king's concubine. But the bloody Krauts have that one. Still, you get the idea.'

'Will I be posing like that—on my front?' I asked. 'My breasts hidden?'

'Oh, for Christ's sake, Magda, you're a grown woman. What's the problem?'

'Nothing. It's just, I've never posed before. I mean,

Victor's the only person who has seen me naked, you know.'

Micheal stared at me, then hooted out a laugh. 'You're a fucking scream, do you know that?' He slapped his palms to his thighs. 'You're thirty-two years of age and Victor Bolding's *all* you've had?' He laughed again. 'My sympathies.'

He continued to snuffle small laughs and I turned back to *L'Odalisque*, my skin pricking.

'That's the kind of woman you understand, Micheal.' I pointed at the painting. 'She's your type. You couldn't care less about real women; three-dimensional ones.'

Micheal folded his palms across his chest and dropped to his knees; the other people in the gallery turned to watch.

'You're smithereening my heart, Mrs Bolding.' He jumped up and grabbed my hand. 'Now, stop the nonsense and come on. We've work to do.'

Micheal's studio in La Ruche was shaped like a triangle of cheese, with the window at the widest end. He had set up a sofa under the window, to represent the *chaise longue* in the painting; I examined its dirty upholstery.

'I'm not lying on that. Get me something to cover it.'

'Your delaying tactics are pissing me off, Magda.' He grimaced, threw down his palette and went to get a coverlet. While he was gone I fuddled out of my dress and underwear; I've always hated undressing in front of people, even Victor. I turned my back to the studio door; Micheal bundled back in with a blanket and pillows from his bed and arranged them on the sofa. 'Now,' he said.

My body felt heavy and cold; I placed my hands on my pouchy belly and glanced over my shoulder at Micheal. He smiled, a gentle smile.

'Will I lie on my stomach?' I asked, and he nodded.

I draped myself over the pillows and breathed the greasy hair smell from them. Micheal came over and arranged my arms and feet. Pushing my face into my hands, I let a groan of embarrassment at the thought of my naked bum being inches from his face.

'Bare flesh is just an ordinary part of the working day for me, Mags, so stop blushing, like a good girl.' He stood back to appraise my position and clapped his hands. 'Right,' he said, pouring himself a glass of white wine, 'let's start.'

My nightdress stayed under the pillow. I let the hotel's cotton sheets tease over my nipples as I slid my body around the bed, letting my legs fall open. While my fingers worked through my soft folds, I thought of Victor. Then Micheal. Then Victor. And I couldn't say who I thought of in the end.

Micheal came to my hotel room. I heard knocking, but no one had knocked on my door before, so I didn't think it was someone looking for me. I lay in bed, trying to fight my way into the morning. Squinting at the sky through the window, I saw a cotton-ball moon suspended in a vapour trail X in the blue sky, like a giant game of x's and o's. The knocking came again.

'*Oui?* Who's there?'

'*C'est moi.* Farrell.'

I jumped up and let him in, then slid back into bed. He came and lay beside me, on top of the covers.

'Her Maj and the boys are coming back tomorrow,' he said. 'You'd better stay away.'

'Until when?'

'For good.' He went up on one elbow and looked down at me. 'She thinks I slept with you. And she's hopping that

9

I didn't get her to pose for the painting.'

I swallowed this news.

'Tell me about Rilke and his wife, Micheal.'

'Not much to tell. They were the proverbial chalk and cheese and should never have gotten together.' He let a short laugh.

'Were they together until the end?'

'No. Rilke offloaded Clara, and their daughter, and went his own way.'

I turned to him and put my arms around his neck; I closed my eyes and gave him a kiss, pressing my mouth to his beer-smelling lips. He flicked his tongue against mine, then pulled away; I opened my eyes.

'Victor says I should come home now,' I said.

Micheal took my arms from his neck and stood up.

'Don't compromise yourself, Magda. You'll turn nasty if you do.' He opened the door, held his hand up in a stiff salute and smiled. 'A bientôt, Madonna Irlanda,' he said, and was gone.

UNMOTHERED

THE OUTFLOW ON the bath is like a keyhole; you stopper it with your toe and let the water lap in your ears, to block out the house. If you were key-shaped, you would slither into that hole and slip down the pipes, away from here. Away from the women who breed women; the women who have cried lavishly for three days, though your daughter was an embarrassment to them and you all know it. When you called your baby Angelica, your sister said it was a waste of a good name.

There is no name for you now. You are wife and sister and daughter and aunt, but you are no longer mother or mammy or mama. If it was you who had died instead of Angelica, she would be called orphan. If it was your husband who had died, he would be a widower. If he were dead, you would be called a widow. But the mother of a dead child is left with nothing; her special name is wiped out with her child's passing.

The long funeral days are over. Angelica's white coffin was lowered into the ground on green ropes. You couldn't help thinking that it looked like a wedding cake, white and smoothly perfect, almost festive. The thought appalled and amused you; it lifted you clear of the snuffling sisters and cousins and colleagues who were huddled at the graveside, stealing your grief. Because of them you couldn't cry.

Your husband holds you in the night, as he held you at the graveyard; you sob and he says, 'It's OK, Claire, everything's going to be fine,' and you wish he would shut up. Platitudes annoy you on a good day; in your sorrow you want to make a ball of every wrong-headed 'It's for the best' and shove it down the speaker's neck. You can't believe that your husband is being so ordinary, so unheartfelt. He has never learnt to feel, you think.

'Nothing is fine,' you scream at him, bucking against his arms, but he stays holding you anyway. His is the kind of love that is unbreakable, like a dam.

Angelica had your husband's eyes: they were an odd milky-blue, like Achill marble. For you, after three years of loving your daughter, they were no longer his eyes, just hers. Everyone admired her eyes; they couldn't find anything else to praise. Her lips listed and drooled; her few teeth were gapped and pointy; her hair was sparse and colourless, like old straw. And she slumped, not able to do much except grunt and roll her unusual eyes. She was your one and only, your baby angel.

You feel like a paper doll; your clothes might as well be held over your shoulders and around your waist by paper tabs. You wouldn't care if your dress fell off and drifted out the door, along the street and slipped down a drain. What do you need clothes for, or food, or drink? What use is anything now?

Your mother-in-law comes to stay when your husband goes back to work.

'You'll go again, Claire, please God, when you're a bit stronger,' she says.

'No. I won't.'

She pours another cup of tea. 'Ah, you will. You'll try again and God will be good to you.'

'I don't want another child. I want Angelica.'

'Well,' she says, 'we'll see.'

You are painting a portrait of a young girl; she is no one you know—you have invented her—and her skin is the same colour as the inside of an oyster shell. Her face almost fills the canvas.

'She doesn't talk to me,' you tell your husband.

He sits in his chair, reading the newspaper and you stand over him.

'Who?'

'The girl, the girl—my portrait.'

'Why do you want her to talk to you?' He lifts his face.

'I didn't say I wanted her to, I just said that she doesn't.' You glare at him. 'They usually talk.'

'Show me the painting,' he says, and you fetch it.

You hold it up and he stares at it. The only bright spot on the canvas is the hint of red in the leaves on a distant tree. Even the girl's eyes are flat and light-drained; her grey dress is sombre.

'What are you thinking?' you ask.

'Portrait of a sick girl,' he says.

Swirling the canvas around, you look at it again. You hadn't thought she might be unwell; just pale, a little under-nourished maybe. Now, looking at your painting, all you see is sickness: wan skin, lips that are too pink, a dead expression. The shadows on the girl's neck make her look even more lifeless. It unnerves you. You put the painting in the cubby under the stairs and crawl in after it, pulling the door behind you. You are hunched on the dust thick floor; the smells are of Hoovered carpet and wellies and old books. The darkness is comforting.

Angelica was no more than a grain of sand once, you think, knocked this way, then that. Pearlising. She gathered you to her, drawing your cells and her father's around her, building herself outwards from you both. She snuggled like a shell-bound sand grain, settling, embedding, readying herself for nearly ten months of growing. But somewhere, somehow, in that miraculous chain, something hiccuped and Angelica became who she was, instead of who you thought she would be.

Your husband paints your portrait in the garden. You are naked, standing in the grass, and every breeze makes your skin prickle. You close your eyes against the sun and feel dizzy when you open them again; you bend to pick the white starflowers that grow all around your toes. You imagine that Angelica is playing in the sandpit, her skin burnt then browned by each passing day. She keeps up a monologue as she plays, instructing an invisible playmate. 'You say this and I say that,' Angelica says. Her voice is clear and high. She runs after a beetle, poking at its back with a twig. Your eyes flick around: from the elderberry bush to the silver-glass globe you have mounted on a stake; from the trailing flowers to the wending pathways. You watch your husband watching you.

Marriage is lonely; you are as alone as you were when you were a child. Your first years of married life were drowned in tears: you cried when you heard music and over soap operas; you cried at a troubled sky. You believed so long in finding a soulmate—Plato's one who makes the other complete—but had finally realised that all you have is yourself, togetherness doesn't make you happy. You let yourself be swallowed up in your husband. But then you ripened like a plum, belly forward, breasts retreating—an exaggeration of the old you—and soon life became even more unrecognisable.

You look at your husband. His brushstrokes are meditative, small; you strain your ears to hear the slap of brush on

canvas—nothing. Sniffing deep on the warm, grassy summer smells, you shut your eyes tight. Your mind sways; you
believe you are here but not here. It's as if you're looking
at yourself, and this life you are anchored in, from somewhere else—a different plane. You pull yourself back and
think of the morning bed.

You like to hear your husband's cry, the deep throated
sound that means he has released his very self into you. You
take his face in your hands and watch his features change
as everything builds up inside him; he always tries to push
his face into your shoulder—you think you distract him
with your inquiring eyes—but you hold his cheeks, keep
his nose a little away from yours, and look at him.

He reddens, begins to thrust quicker, and the skin pulls
across his cheekbones; his mouth opens wide then wider,
his head tilts back. He looks at you as if from a great distance; you wonder if he can see you. His movements
become fast, distracted, instinctive, and then the words
come: 'Oh, my love, oh, Claire, I love you, I love you', and
his lips fall to your mouth for deep kisses. When his eyes
open to yours—slowly, glazed over—he drinks you in and
smiles. You lie under him and wonder if you love him, or
what love is at all.

It has been six months. Your husband thinks you should get
a job; and he wants to start going out again. You don't want
to go anywhere but he arranges a dinner with old friends
and you agree to it.

'Here comes Jim with his little Claire under his arm.'
Daniel tosses the remark over his shoulder to his wife
Róisín as you walk up their driveway.

'I heard that,' you say, and Daniel looks at the ground, laughs, then grunts.

Róisín comes out the door and walks towards you with her arms wide; you endure a brittle hug. She holds you away from her.

'I'm so sorry about your little girl, Claire.'

She doesn't even remember Angelica's name. 'Thanks, Róisín,' you say.

You don't want to talk about any of it and you're glad when she claps her hands together and says, 'Wine!' She ushers everyone into the house and queens it over you, as usual; you think she takes your reserve for gormlessness. She fills your wine glass. 'Drink up, Claire, for God's sake. You need it.'

Their house is better than yours; the dining room has brindled wallpaper that reminds you of ancient leopard-skin and the shelves are weighty with glass and silver. One of their sofas is shaped like a pair of pillowed lips.

You watch Róisín flirt with your husband, lunging her cleavage under his nose. She doesn't catch his indifference; you could tell her he notices nothing and save her the effort, but why bother? You wonder then what you are doing here; why your husband keeps up this friendship that is based on nothing; why you are not at home, safe on your own sofa. You look at Daniel, thinking you would like to climb on top of him and show him what you can do. He's looking at you over the rim of his glass and you like how it makes you feel: squirmy and at least half-alive.

You are not able to flirt; you're too self-conscious to throw yourself at men and, being married, it seems pointlessly complicated. But Daniel. Well, despite his cruel remark earlier, he has always seemed like a man who might make you happy. He does nothing for his wife; she's too mired in her manic need to be enjoyed to care about her husband. He looks neglected; you'd say what Daniel needs is a surprising, generous fuck.

You are in the kitchen, you and Daniel. You're rinsing shot glasses and he's drying them, sticking a long, tea towel-wrapped finger into each one, and swirling it. You can hear his wife's plangent plong-plong from the other room; she is falling over your husband with another of her self-starring anecdotes.

'Sherry increases my loquacity,' you hear her hoot, in a mocking voice.

Daniel throws you a half-smile. 'Her mother always says that.' His teeth have nicotined stripes; you like the way they look. 'How are you doing, Claire?'

You shrug. 'OK, I suppose.'

'It must be very hard.'

'It is.' He takes another clean glass from your hand. 'She used to laugh in her sleep you know, Angelica did. It was the only time she sounded like any other little girl.'

'She was having happy dreams,' he says.

You nod. 'That's what I always thought.'

You stop the wash-and-dry routine and stare at each other. Your face is sweat-lagged from the scalding sink water; heat has swooned to your armpits and under your breasts. Daniel leans over and kisses you, his tongue as liquid and swollen as your own. You kiss him back, not bothering to wipe the slew of dribble that coats your chins. His kiss is demanding and sweet. You pull back and, with wet fingers, unbutton the top of his shirt and press your nose onto his chest; his skin smells like cucumber.

'Are we starting something?' you ask, lifting your eyes to his.

He grabs your head and kisses you again; the shot glass

that is still thimbled on his finger digs into your skull.

'Hurry up in there, Claire,' Róisín calls, 'or you never know what I'll do to this gorgeous man of yours.' She cackles.

Daniel holds you to him, then releases you. He kisses your forehead and puts the shot glasses and a bottle of tequila on a plastic tray.

'We'll be together,' he says.

You follow him into the sitting room, where Róisín is slow-dancing with your husband to no music at all.

TO DRIFT AND TO LIFT

THE AIR SLUNG like a noose around my nose and mouth, then slipped down to settle on my neck. I had never felt as uncomfortable in my own skin; the flabby heat made my trousers stick to my legs like flypaper. I craved two things: water to drink and breathable air. The Hotel Bright, when I got there after a bumpy auto-rickshaw ride, was anything but. My room was dim and plain; it made the squalid chalets from childhood trips to Butlin's holiday camp look five-star. But, seeing a merry parade of sadhus under my balcony, all of them slung with saffron garlands and moving to a brass band, made me feel a little less dark. Watching the procession pass, I let the bone-weariness that always comes over me after a long journey descend into my body.

From the balcony I could see a woman selling bananas at the corner of the square; she kept her head low and her fingers twitched at the hem of her sari. A baby wriggled on a cloth on the ground beside her. My heart leapt with some unnameable pain and I turned away to survey my bedroom again. The word simple was too elaborate. Barren, I thought, this room is barren. I looked over at the banana seller and her child once more, then threw myself down onto the inch-thin mattress. Lying there, waiting for the dark, I heard the slow start of heavy rain and I wanted to cry. One long, wearying day and already I was both frightened and bewitched by India.

All night I listened to convulsive weeping from the room next door; two or three voices shared the sobbing and wailing; I wondered if they were in mourning. I slept towards dawn, then got up and ran through a downpour to Lords Café for breakfast. Sitting in a window seat, I had peaches, Darjeeling tea and a boiled egg. Delhi looked different under rain: even more chaotic and crowded than the previous day's dust-caked incarnation. After eating, I went out to look for a telephone, to let the Foundation know that I had arrived. It was hard to get used to the mêlée on the streets and the endless, huge-eyed children who pulled at me as I walked, begging for a few rupees. Men and women stared at me and I couldn't help feeling a bit foolish. I found a phone on a side street and dialled the number I had been given. A man answered.

'Hello, can I speak to Meera, please?' I said.

'I speak.'

'This is Marcus Fitzgerald here, from Ireland. Would Meera be there at all?' I fumbled with the letter I'd been sent. 'Or Shanthi?'

'I speak. No Shanthi. School,' he said. Silence, then: 'Yes, Mr Marky.'

'My name is Marcus. Mr Marcus Fitzgerald. I am from Ireland.' I spoke clearly. 'I have come to volunteer? At one of the schools?' More silence. 'Hello, are you there?'

'Yes, many volunteer come,' the man said, and then he hung up.

'OK . . .' I said, into the receiver, and decided I would go to the Foundation's city office to see what was what.

I was driven in an auto-rickshaw from the office to the school I had been assigned to. The school was in a village of tin-box shops, stone huts with painted shutters, carts strapped onto weary oxen, pigs snuffling in debris and the usual gaggle of staring people. The clusters of flies and the claggy heat irritated me. When I stepped out of the rickshaw, giggling children horded around me, hiding their faces and sneaking peeps at my face; I felt like a piss-pale giant among Lilliputians. I flapped my hands like a lunatic, trying to get the flies to stop buzzing around my eyes and nose. This made the boys and girls laugh more.

A woman—who was not much bigger than the children —introduced herself as Shanthi; she smiled, showing huge, crooked teeth. A younger man, who batted flies from his face with a lazy swish of the arm, lingered close to Shanthi and watched me.

'Welcome, Marcus Fitzgerald,' Shanthi said, 'I am glad to meet you.' She introduced the man as Pandu; he nodded and did not smile when I held out my hand to him. 'Dinner first, then a rest. Tomorrow we will show you the video about our work and introduce you to our school.'

I followed her through a dining hall that had three long tables, looking forward to tasting the spicy food that I could smell. Shanthi lead me to a small room where, apparently, I was to eat alone. She left and Pandu brought me a platter with potatoes, eggs, sweating tomatoes and sliced raw onion. He stood watching me eat and, every so often, I looked over at him.

'The food is good. Very good,' I said; I hoped he would leave.

Pandu stared at me, his black eyes steady. The potatoes and eggs were bland, saltless, and I could catch the curling aroma of garam masala or some other spice blend. I turned when I heard scrabbling noises, hoping Shanthi had come back, and saw a rat poking its snout under the door.

'Jesus!' I jumped from my seat. Pandu grinned and stamped his foot; the rat scuffled off to nose somewhere else. 'That frightened the shite out of me. I can't stand rats,' I said, my heart walloping in my chest. 'I suppose no one can.' Sitting back down, I looked at Pandu. 'So, are you from Delhi?'

'Udaipur,' he said.

'Oh, I'm going to go there next, when I've finished here. What's it like?'

Pandu shrugged, folded his hands behind his back like a sentry, and stared at me again. I held his gaze for a moment, then turned away and finished eating my food.

The next morning, after watching an information video, Shanthi got us some chai and we sat on a bench in the school-yard to drink it. The sun burnt down and made everything hot to touch: my hair, the seat, the ground. I had not slept well in my stone hut.

'You had a good sleep, Marcus?' Shanthi said.

'Oh, yes.'

She poured the milky chai into two earthenware cups; I blew on it and watched the film on its surface break up, like waves dying on a shore.

'Did you enjoy the information video, Marcus?'

I liked the way Shanthi pronounced my name, making a short roll on the 'r'; she spoke haltingly, as if choosing each of her words with real care. Her face was perfect, like a Bollywood heroine's, until she smiled and revealed her bucked teeth. Still, she was beautiful, and I wondered why women were nearly always good-looking in some way; it seemed a reversal of the peacocks-in-nature law.

'Marcus?'

'The film was emotional, really,' I said, 'but in a good way. The children's lives obviously improve tenfold once they come to the school.'

'Their whole families' lives improve,' she said. 'Even though some parents hate that the children are not earning money, for the long term it is good. For everyone.'

We sipped at the sweet chai. I looked at Shanthi and she looked back at me; we stayed like that, neither of us turning away, until we heard Pandu shout. He was skittering around the yard, lining up the children to perform for us.

'We are ready,' he called. 'Shanthi! The children are ready now.'

They stood in a wide half-circle; the girls had neat shirt-waist dresses, and plaits folded into rings and tied with ribbons. The boys were like younger versions of the village men: thin, wide-mouthed, open, with shucks of uneven black hair. They all made namaste to us, giggling the greeting and hiding their faces in the bow. Then they sang, danced, and put on a short play about a courtship. When they had finished, they ran to where Shanthi and I were sitting. Some snuggled into her lap, whispering and pulling at her long black plait and touching her neck with their slim brown fingers.

'The children want you to sing a song from your country,' she said.

I sang 'Molly Malone' because it was all I could think of: "*Crying cockles and mussels, alive, alive-o*". The children clapped and laughed, and I blushed because I had sung such a bad song so badly.

'Something by Madonna now,' Shanthi said, on instruction from the children.

'Like a Virgin', popped into my head; nothing else. 'I don't know any songs by Madonna,' I said.

Through Shanthi, they asked if I was married. I said that I was single and I was pronounced too old to be wifeless.

'The girls and boys want to know why your skin is "white like a pig",' Shanthi said, holding her hand to her mouth and laughing.

They wanted to know if there were child labourers in Ireland, or if all children studied there. One serious-eyed boy held my hand through all of these enquiries and hugged me hard when I stood up. I shook his hand and patted his back, feeling a bit tearful.

'He has no parents,' Shanthi said.

'It's terrible,' I said, really meaning it, though, to my own ears I sounded insincere. 'Do you have children?' I asked her.

'My husband and I have not been blessed with offspring,' she said, looking away.

The stiffness of her answer kept me quiet as she showed me around the rest of the school. I was assigned the D class, which was made up of new children. They were sober in their seats and some of them held toddlers in their laps—they were in their charge, Shanthi explained, while their parents begged or worked.

'Teach them their A,B,C's, sing to them and play with them. I will come by each day to see you all and make sure you are getting along just fine.' Shanthi grinned.

'Hello, everyone,' I said to the children, and a flock of cowed faces looked up at me.

'Give them a little English and a lot of air and fun, Marcus,' she said, 'we want them to keep coming back.'

I was lying under a tree in the dust, eyes closed, enjoying the shade, listening to The Shambirds on my iPod. After two weeks of on-off power cuts, I had finally managed to charge it up and I was loving the comfort of the familiar music. The song lifted and drifted and I could hear a smile in the singer's voice—she suddenly sounded brighter. I wondered what had happened in the recording studio to make her happy. Just the singing of the song, maybe.

Sensing that someone was standing over me, I opened my eyes to see Shanthi. I pulled the earphones from my ears and said, 'Hello.'

'Ireland is an island,' she said, scratching the toe of her sandal through the dust.

'That's right.' I sat up and patted the space beside me; she lowered herself to the ground opposite me in one concertina fold.

'I looked at it on the map.'

I nodded. 'Where are you from, Shanthi?'

'Here. I was born and raised in New Delhi.'

'And your husband?'

'Naveen is from the south. Bangalore. He goes there often to see his mother; he is there now.' She pointed at my iPod; it was still churning out songs in a tin-canny way. 'May I listen?'

'Sure.' I plugged her into the music, letting my fingers linger on her soft lobes and the antique gold of her earrings. 'They're an Irish band,' I said, though she couldn't hear me. I leaned forward, unpopped one earphone and said, 'Irish folk-rock', indicating the iPod.

Shanthi nodded and cast one of her sudden, toothy smiles at me. Sitting back in the dust, I watched her tentative swaying to the music. She smiled hugely and clicked her fingers, and I felt happy.

I heard a knock and I knew it was Shanthi; I could nearly feel the slide of her knuckle against the door, the jut of wood on her tiny, perfect bones. I had just come up from the shower room and was standing in the middle of the floor, trying to decide which T-shirt might be clean enough to wear. She would have seen me, towel-wrapped and wet-backed, flip-flopping into my hut; she rapped again.

'I'm in my pelt—hang on a second!' I shouted, but she had already opened the door and was halfway across the room, hitching her cinnamon sari over her shoulder. Shanthi didn't say anything but put her arms around my waist and dropped her palms to cup my bum. Her cheek was warm against my chest; I lifted her chin and bent my lips to hers.

'No, Marcus,' she said, turning her face away. Her fingers slid up my arms. 'What is this for?' She had landed on my tattoo. 'Why "Mum"?'

I fingered the tattoo. 'It's an old-fashioned design, kind of ironic: the heart and the dagger and "Mum". My mother hated it—she said it was common.' I laughed. 'But she died a few months after I got it, so I'm glad I have it.'

'I am sorry your mother passed on. Really, Marcus, I am.'

I nodded and she continued to hold me, humming some unknown tune to herself and rocking us both. Her fingers roved from my arms to the small of my back to my bum cheeks, circling and squeezing. My cock stiffened and I sighed. Winding her plait around one hand, I petted her neck with the other.

Shanthi was the smallest woman I had ever known. I wanted to lift her tiny-as-a-hummingbird body and place it under me on the narrow bed; I would unpeel her from her sari and pass my hands over every furl of her honey-flesh. With my lips, I wanted to taste and coax her until she quivered. I would enter her slowly and love her carefully. But I knew she would not allow any of it and I couldn't push her.

'Can I kiss you, Shanthi?'

She shook her head and looked up at me, halfway, it seemed, between tears and a smile, then pulled herself out of my arms and left the room. I heard her greet someone in the yard, her voice light and tense, and I stayed where I was, swaying in the dusk-dark.

'Describe snow to me,' Shanthi said.

I was sitting on the floor of my hut with my back to the wall and she was tucked like a child between my legs. School was over and she had stayed on into the evening, doing paperwork. Hoping she would come to me, I had waited, sitting in the dark of my room, hour after hour, until she opened my door and came in. She settled her back against my stomach, wriggling in tight, as if she was waiting to hear a long-loved bedtime story. With one finger, I traced the pathway of her hair-parting—it cleaved through her hair like veining through black marble.

'Snow? Well, it can look different depending on how it falls: sometimes it's powdery like dandruff, sometimes thick like milk.' Shanthi laughed. 'And it's never really white: it's violet, blue, shiny like diamonds, grey. Snow is extra cold—colder than this wall here,' I said, pushing her hand against the stone. 'It's soft to touch, it melts away under your fingers, but you can pack it together and make it as hard as rock.'

'Like magic.'

'A bit like magic,' I said, smoothing the back of her hair with my palms.

'Now, the ocean. Tell me what that looks like.'

'The ocean! That's such a big word, an American word. I always call it the sea.' I thought for a few seconds. 'The sea is wider than the widest river you've ever seen and the water is bright, unmuddy. The shore is golden and the water looks like lace, breaking over the sand.' I placed my hands on her thighs and she didn't lift them off, though I thought she would. 'The sea needs lots of 's' words to describe it: splashing, sand, shells, spades, spray, slapping, shimmering, shoals, starfish, sailing boats, swordfish, seals, shipwrecks, stingrays.' I was out of breath. 'And sharks,' I said, mock-biting her legs with my fingers.

'Marcus! Say how the ocean *looks*, please,' she said, poking my knees.

'The sea, the sea, the sea.' I spoke quickly: 'It's as huge as the sky, as green as phlegm, as blue as turquoise, it's dark like thunderclouds, as dangerous as war.' I paused, lifted my fingers into the heat of her armpits. '*She sells seashells on the seashore.*' I laughed and said it faster, into her curved ear. '*She sells seashells on the seashore.*' Shanthi giggled —a low, gurgling, giddy sound. 'You have to tell *me* things now. About India. About you.'

'What things?' she asked.

'I don't know. Well, what does your name mean, for a start?'

'Shanthi? It means "peace".'

'It suits you. It suits you very well.' I hugged her to me, my hands glancing the soft swell of her breasts, and I lowered my lips to nip her neck. As soon as she felt my mouth on her skin, she twisted away from me and stood up. Shanthi pressed her hands over the skirt of her sari like a cook smoothing her apron.

'I have to go.'

'Always leaving,' I said.

'Yes, I am always leaving.' She smiled down at me, pulling her dark lips back from her porcelain teeth—the only big thing about her—and ran to the door.

Pandu came to my hut; he knocked on the window shutters and I opened them.

'Her husband is back from Bangalore,' he said.

'Is he really?' I looked past him to the yard where the

children were standing in a circle, tossing a deflated leather ball from one to another. The dust around them made them look like half-people, existing only from the waist up.

'Yes, Marcus. It is serious. Shanthi must not come to you anymore.'

I stared at him. 'What do you mean "come to" me?'

He frowned. 'Marcus, perhaps it is now time you left for Udaipur.'

'Don't tell me what to do, Pandu.' I grabbed the shutters, forcing him to move back quickly, and closed them against him.

During the night there was a scrabbling under my door. I stacked bricks against it every bedtime to keep the rats away but they still got in sometimes—I had found their pellets in my rucksack and gnaw marks on a packet of nuts; I had stopped keeping food in my hut after that. I hated the rats even more than the flies—they were plump and casual and ever-present. The scratching noise didn't last, so I thought the rat must have got fed up rummaging against the wall of bricks and gone away. I fell back asleep, feeling triumphant. In the morning, there was a folded piece of paper on the floor behind my brick-stack; it was a used train ticket: 'Pushkar Travels, Bangalore to Delhi', it said. Turning it over I found square, block-capitalled writing: I HAVE NEVER LOVED ANY OTHER.

Shanthi did not come to my class that day. I was only half with the children and we spent most of the day in the yard, throwing a ball and playing chasing, so that I could keep one eye on her office. When the children were at their afternoon meal, Pandu came to my classroom. He stood in the doorway but I didn't turn to him until he called out to me.

'Hey, Marcus,' he said, and I looked over. 'Naveen has

taken her to Bangalore.' He smiled. 'And she will not be back.'

Pandu snorted a laugh and went back out into the yard. I could still hear him laughing somewhere close by while the D class trooped back in and took their seats.

EKPHRASIS

Édouard Manet
Le Déjeuner sur l'Herbe, 1863

She has a doughy face and bulging, raisin eyes; her belly-folds flop one over another in a fleshy heap. Her companions look like Mediterraneans trying to be gentlemen, with their succulent lips, hirsute chins and cheap jackets.

This is no nude; she brazens at me from the painting, a naked, living woman. There is hair (hair!) peeking from her armpit, and the sole of one lumpen foot bares itself to my eyes. Her dress, a discarded picnic blanket of blue silk-organza, holds—instead of the meat of her—a tilted basket of peaches, plums and grapes, as well as a water flask and a knot of bread.

Another woman—the last quarter, I presume, of this vulgar foursome—is paddling in murky water in the background. She, at least, has remained half-clothed and retains something of the aura of a wood nymph among dark trees.

But her naked sister, well, she is a wanton, who clearly has been, or shortly will be, *in flagrante delicto* with her swarthy suitors. And I've no doubt, from the cut of her jib, that indeed she would welcome onlookers.

31

NUDE

Pablo Picasso
Le Déjeuner sur l'Herbe
(d'après Édouard Manet), 1960

Yeah, it's hard to know what Picasso was up to with this, really. Is it homage or piss-take? Either way, it's great. The nude is flat-white and she's shaped like a cello—she seems to be playing herself with a bow. Deeper meaning?

There's only one man, the other clearly didn't show up. The man who is there, though, seems to have brought along an attractive glass triangle. Hey, early inspiration for I. M. Pei's Louvre pyramid!

Something on the front right of the scene has caught the nude's interest: it might be one of the limes/lemons/grapefruit. Is she hungry, or suffering from scurvy and therefore craving the juicy citrus flesh? Or she may want to nab her frock from under the fruit and that shell-like, cabbagey thing, so that she can dress and leave.

The background trees are a fern-frondy canopy and the woman in the (cerulean) water has pneumatic—if lopsided —boobs, and (perhaps) no head.

I don't think the nude and the man are planning anything. They don't seem that interested in each other.

Bow Wow Wow
See Jungle! See Jungle! Go Join Your Gang, Yeah, City All Over! Go Ape Crazy!
(LP cover, after Édouard Manet), 1981

Annabella Lwin. Starkers on the front of the album. She was only fourteen when that pic was taken and her mother went ape, crazy, doo-lally. Mine would've too. Still, it's deadly. She's bloody perfect, of course, all tanned and flat stomached. Her real name is like Myan Myan Mar or something;

she's from the Burmese jungle, I heard. Hence the tan. Anyway, Bow Wow Wow's manager said she'd never get anywhere in the music biz with a mad name like Mar Mar, or whatever it was, so he changed it. *He* changed it, not her!

The picture? Oh, yeah, sorry . . . It's nice, summery. They might be having a picnic but all they have is a few apples and oranges, it looks like. It's a very green photo—even the water is green—but there's brown muck near the front and they guy leaning down on the right is wearing red trousers; that adds a lot of colour. And the boat is red too. I think the woman in the water is black; she has a turban on her head.

Annabella's skin is very bright. She looks out from the photograph and the two guys just chat to each other. The three of them make a triangle. Is that enough? Oh, when they released 'Go Wild in the Country' as a single, they put the same photo in black and white on the cover, but it didn't look as good. 'I Want Candy' is still their best song, I think.

AN AMARNA PRINCESS UP
NORTH

THE POLICE WASN'T that interested in why I done it, more like *how*. They asked me loads of questions and I tried to be honest but, you know.

They says to me, 'You're a fantasist, Shine.'

And I'm like, 'I am not.'

It was all questions: 'What training have you had, Oscar? Did you always make things, Oscar? What school were you at?'

I said, 'I had no training, I didn't go to no art school. I like the library. A bit boring, aren't I?'

'No,' said the Art Squad fella, 'you're very interesting to us Oscar Shine, as it happens.'

The ones in the British Museum called my Dad 'Old Moon-Shine'. That's rude, innit? My Mam was Kathleen to them, or Missus Shine, but they didn't respect her enough either. Dad went with the silver chalice to the British Museum; he sold it to them and we got a few bob. He told them his grandmother owned it and she used polish it, and his little self weren't allowed to touch it. I loved making that chalice in my shed—melting the silver, casting the scene with the hart and the hunters, getting it all perfect —it were like telling myself a story.

Dad were always great for a yarn; he could tell you anything and make you believe it were fact and true, something that happened. Ever since I were a kid he'd tell me about how things have history, real and made-up, and that it's what we feel about those things that counts. Don't matter what other people think. Just you.

Dad showed me a box of pointy stones once, when I were a lad.

'What are them?' I said.

'Arrowheads. From the Stone Age,' Dad said. I lifted one and ran my finger down its edge. He watched, fixing his green eye on me. 'Do you believe that, Oscar?' he said.

'Yes.'

Dad slapped my ear and it zinged. He laughed, a short laugh. 'I made them, you daft dolt.' He grabbed the arrowhead and put the lid back on the box. 'It's not important what's true, Oscar. The truth is an illusion, innit?'

That's what he liked to say.

Me and Dad would go to auctions and buy bits and bobs, then we'd oldify them—a sup of tea on a map, an ancient frame on a new picture. Then Mam would put on her best frock and go to the antique shops and sell them. We got right good at the whole game. The thing was, I wanted to paint, only Dad kept saying that were a waste of time and money. But I painted anyway, in my shed, late at night. And I tried to sell a few of my pictures around, but nobody were interested. If what I had to sell were something ancient, or it had a name to it, they were all eyes and ears, but nobody wanted new, original stuff. Dad looked over my paintings and said they were good though.

'You can draw, son,' he said, and I were proud.

So we put together a plan.

The silver chalice were the first thing I made. After that it were right easy to come up with things to do. Into the library for ideas and information. Down to B&Q for the tools. Over to Mattie's Salvage in the Rover for stone or marble or timber. A chat with Dad. A chat with Mam. Then all were ready: I made statues, stone panels, chalices, carved reliefs of men, women and feasts. You name it. And I painted too.

Them were happy years: carving, painting and creating in my shed. On my own with dust and oil paint filling up my nose and tickling down my throat. Pots of brushes on every shelf, rolls of canvas by the door, a kiln and a printing press tucked in the cupboards. Limestone, glass and marble, here, there and everywhere.

The selling were Mam and Dad's job; that's what they were experts at. They could invent a relative at a second's notice: we were related to L.S. Lowry, Henry Moore the sculptor, and all sorts; Paul Gauguin were a pal of a French granny of mine. Mam and Dad could convince, you see, just by being humble and ordinary and old. That were the trick.

But I had in my head to do something big. I wanted to try a marble statue, one I'd read about in an Egyptology book: *Nefertiti's daughter, Tutunkhamun's sister—The Amarna Princess*. I fell in love with her, didn't I? The white woman. The perfect, smooth calmness of her; the woman who'd never turn her back or slit her eyes at me, like the girls in the paper shop. She'd be the woman who'd expect nothing of Oscar Shine.

I called Mam and Dad down to the shed.

'How about this?' I said.

Mam looked at my sketch. 'She's got no bloody head, Oscar,' she said, 'what use is she?' Mam squinted. 'No. I don't like that.'

But Dad could see the potential. Already he were making up the back story, where the statue had come from, how we'd got hold of her. I could see his cogs turning from where I sat. But it were Mam—Mam who already hated my Princess—who pulled the rabbit out of the sack. The masterstroke.

'She rings a bell, so she does. That name. Amarna,' she said, twisting her hands together, and she went off up to the house. Dad and me looked at the sketch of the Princess and made plans.

'You'll want to use alabaster,' Dad said. 'That'll do rightly.'

Mam came back and she were grinning like a mare, a book in her hands. She tossed it to Dad. 'Look at that,' she said.

' "Plimpton Demesne, 1873",' Dad read, off the front of the book. It were an auctioneer's catalogue. He flicked through to where Mam showed him and whistled. 'Boy, oh boy, Kathleen,' he said. 'Boy, oh bloody boy.'

The catalogue had an Amarna Princess among the items listed for sale. We had our provenance.

We were together for three weeks. I chipped her out of alabaster, slinking in ginger lines with the hand chisel, being careful not to bruise the stone; using the riffler when I wanted to smooth her down. I made her body light and airy. You could see the graining in the stone and she were luminous, like opal. I carved her breasts, her pot belly, her wide thighs and the V between them. I veiled her in lined gossamer—a gentle covering for all the parts of her that I'd created.

I sang to her when the house were in bed; I don't have much of a voice, but if I croon low it don't sound too bad. I sang that Coldplay song 'Yellow', because it's about a chap who loves a girl. He says her skin and bones turn into something beautiful and that's what I were doing: turning my princess into a beautiful thing, an invented thing, my own girl.

I carved her head; I made it a part of her and then I had to knock it off. I kept it, of course. It were that stunning, what else could I do? I gave her a black woman's gorgeous lips; hair that pointed backwards like a newborn's skull; and huge, placid eyes. Then I took my mallet to her swan neck and whacked until her eyes stared up at me from the shed floor. I looked at her down there and had a little cry, then I wrapped the head in a blanket and shoved it into the cupboard. That near broke me.

Dad said we should go local with this one. Be audacious. Mam and me weren't sure at first but then I said, 'Fuck it', so we did. The chap at the local museum sent a lady out to the house. Dad pulled the bust of the Amarna Princess out from under the stairs and unwrapped her from the beach towel he'd put around her.

'My old father owned it, brought it back from the Continent. A dealer said he'd give me five hundred pound for it,' Dad said. 'Thought maybe it might be worth more when he said that. But I'll put it in the garden if it's worth nothing. I'm not that fond of it.'

'The head's missing,' Mam said.

The lady knelt on the floor, looked over the Princess, and all but hugged her. Dad showed her the auction catalogue and she nearly peed herself then and there.

'I can tell you, Mister Shine, that this is a pre-eminent object, over two thousand years old, and we at the Museum will be most happy to purchase it. Most happy.' She were red and smiling.

I couldn't smile; I didn't want the Princess to go. That weren't a thing I could say to Dad though.

Queen Elizabeth came to visit my Princess at the

Museum where she were the centrepiece of the their Ancient World collection. One royal lady come to pay respects to another. We got nearly half a million pound for the Princess, after Sotheby's said she were the real deal but, to me, she were worth more. Not in a money way, in the other way.

I went to see her at the Museum and sang a bit of the Yellow song to her, real quiet.

'For you I'd bleed myself dry,' I whispered.

But it weren't the same because she were stuck behind glass, and I were stuck outside it, and it were like being at the zoo, not able to touch, so I went home.

Dad were never in a wheelchair before the court case. He told the judge he got bullets in his spine during the Italian campaign near Lucca. Thing is, Dad never went to war. He were a deserter. That's what Mam told me when she came to see me on visiting day last week. There's a lot mixed up about Dad.

The police asked so many questions. Thirty hours of bloody questions, with that chap from the Art Squad.

'Is it true, Oscar, that you used tea to age the Amarna Princess?'

'Tea and mud,' I said.

'Do you know you used the wrong stone, the wrong material?'

'Wiltshire stone, it were.' I shrugged. 'Fooled most of the experts though, didn't it?' I looked at my hands. 'I just have to do this for some reason, I don't know. I've said all I can say. It's my fault. I'll take the rap.'

'The man who rumbled you wasn't fooled though, was he? "Don't make me laugh." That's what he said when he saw your Princess.'

'Whatever,' I said.

'You made a lot of money over the years, Oscar. Why did you live like a pauper?'

'I've got six pair of socks, never worn. What more do I want?'

I'm glad Mam and Dad are safe at home. Glad all the asking is over. But, you see, the police missed one thing. The real reason why I did it. The reason I couldn't stop.

I'm an artist, see. I have to make art. That's what they missed.

MRS MORISON OF HADDO

I WEAR THE BLUE silk gown for my portrait, with a lace capelet and my marriage pearls. In painting a half-portrait, Ramsay, the artist, accommodates my wish to hide the swell of my belly. I am all amazement that he consults me concerning the making of the portrait. He says my comfort is the most important thing, for only when I am at ease will he 'capture my essence'.

'My style is natural, Madam,' he says, 'and your husband is fond of nature.'

'He is, Sir,' I agree, thinking of the nights Mr Morison enters my bedchamber, scatters the bedclothes and then enters myself. The thought sends flushes to my face and I glance at Ramsay. He leaps suddenly from behind his easel and I too leap. 'Mr Ramsay?' I say, hurrying to stand behind my chair. The babe I am carrying quickens with fright.

Ramsay stops, fumbles in his waistcoat pocket, then holds two blue feathers aloft, like a man surrendering. 'For your hair, Madam; to balance the colour in my painting.'

I sit, relieved. ' "*My* painting", you say, Mr Ramsay? Surely the painting is mine and Mr Morison's?' I like teasing him; I nod, to signal that he may approach me.

The heft of his body hovers beside my face while he fixes the feathers into my hair; I smell rain from him and paint and linseed. And something else: that peculiar masculine musk which reminds me of red wine.

'I would like a daughter, but Mr Morison, of course, wants a son.' It is ridiculous to reveal my heart, but some foolishness has entered my spirit.

41

NUDE

'Naturally you crave the company of your sex, Madam,' Ramsay says.

I breathe deep on his smell, catch his hands in mine and kiss them. He pulls free, walks back to his easel and begins.

COWBOY AND NELLY

TWO DAYS AFTER Cowboy met Nelly, he had her name tattooed on the white skin of his inner wrist. The girl who inked the tattoo stayed silent. Cowboy wanted to talk; he wanted to tell the girl about Nelly, about her jutting clavicle and mannish hands, about her sweet-dough smell. But once he had talked to the tattooist about what he wanted her to draw, she didn't speak again.

Cowboy was worried that the script might blur if the letters were tiny and crowded.

'Don't make the name too small,' he said, trying to sound calm.

The tattooist nodded and continued to inscribe Nelly's name in a line of plain, purple letters. Outside the tattoo parlour, Cowboy stripped the bandage from his wrist, held his arm up under a street lamp on O'Connell Street, and whispered, 'Nelly'.

He couldn't tell if Nelly liked the tattoo when he showed it to her in The Cova that night; her face didn't change when she took his arm and held her hand under his, palm up, like a communicant waiting for the host. She squinted at the tattoo, lifted Cowboy's arm nearer to her eyes, then pushed it away.

'It's not even my real name,' she said.

Cowboy stretched his wrist and looked at the tattoo.

'What is your real name then?'

Nelly sipped her beer. 'Helen.'

'And who calls you Helen?'

'No one. Well, no one that counts.'

'Then Nelly *is* your real name,' Cowboy said, and tucked his arm over her shoulder, pulling her along the bench to cradle her body into his. He dropped his mouth to her head and smelt his own underarm sweat and the yeastiness of Nelly's hair.

Three months after Cowboy met Nelly, they got married. Their agreements for the marriage were simple: no children; no secrets. Cowboy wore gold-plated collar tips and a bolo tie that he had sent all the way from New Mexico. Nelly wore her sister Maureen's wedding dress; she did not like waste and didn't mind that the dress was yellowing and out of style by a few years. They met outside the registrar's office in the rain and, in that dress, Cowboy thought Nelly was the loveliest thing he had ever seen.

'You look smashing, babe,' he whispered, 'sexy.'

'I'll do,' Nelly said, and crooked her arm into his.

Maureen and her husband Liam were the witnesses.

After the ceremony Maureen said, 'Not much of a marriage without a priest.'

Nelly leaned up and kissed Cowboy on the mouth and said, 'Let's go.'

Cowboy thought Maureen and Liam would never leave, after the four of them had eaten pork and vegetables enough for ten people in an empty restaurant. He wanted to get Nelly back to the hotel, so they would get good use out of the papery sheets, the bath, and all the stations on the television. He could hardly wait to feel the heat of the room and the naked weight of Nelly in his arms.

'We'll be off now, Helen,' Maureen said, when the conversation had been deader than dead for more than an hour.

'Grand,' said Nelly. 'We want to get to the hotel anyway.

44

To see how we get on.'

Liam winked at Cowboy and sniggered. Cowboy felt like thumping him but, on some signal of their own, Liam and Maureen got up abruptly and walked away, leaving the newlyweds alone at the table.

'Cheerio now,' Liam called over his shoulder, without looking back. His voice sounded too smart for Cowboy's ears.

'I've seen happier corpses than that pair,' Cowboy said, and they both laughed.

'Thank fuck they're gone,' Nelly said; she put her head on his lap and sighed.

That night, in the hotel on Talbot Street, Nelly took the meat and muscle of her new husband into every open part of her. Cowboy slid over and around and under her, grabbing and sucking and moving until he was sore. He relished the heavy velvet of her skin on and under him. They cried in each other's arms in the early morning hours with the relief and joy of love. Afterwards Cowboy watched Nelly sleeping; he admired her long jaw and the way her hair curled around her ears.

A year after Cowboy married Nelly, he took the bus into town to buy her an anniversary present. He sloped up Thomas Street, high on the smell of over-ripe fruit and Daz. The street sellers called out to him: 'Do you want any washing powder, son?' 'Ten for a euro the juicy mandarins. Do you want mandarins, love?' Cowboy smiled, shook his head and went into Frawley's. He had always liked the fresh chaos of drapery shops: the rolls of oilcloth, the baskets of knickers, the clutter of shirts and dresses that hung in thin plastic covers; everything smelled promising and new.

He stood in the middle of the shop floor, wondering

what Nelly might need. Seeing a rack of sherbet coloured nightdresses, he thought one of them would be just the thing. He went over and fingered each of the nightdresses, eventually lifting down a short peach one. Cowboy held it up against himself and looked in a mirror; he swayed a little, imagining the lace collar against Nelly's throat. He felt eyes watching him; he turned and saw Maureen.

Cowboy had always had a sense of his own foolishness; it wasn't his long, skinny body, or his western hat or boots, though they did not fit in with the tracksuits and sweat shirts everyone else wore. He saw something else reflected back at him from other people: a kind of scorn that made him feel like he could not belong. Nelly never looked at him like that—she took him for what he was—but around Maureen, Cowboy felt wary and stupid.

'Well,' she said. 'There you are.'

'Hello Maureen. Out shopping, are you?'

'Window-shopping more like. Is that nightdress for Helen? It won't fit her.' She grabbed at the material of the nightie and tossed it from her fingers as if it was greasy.

'We're a year married tomorrow.'

Maureen snorted. 'Pretend married.' She grabbed a blue floor-length nightdress from the rack and shoved it at Cowboy. 'Get her this one.'

Cowboy watched Maureen trot away and out the door of the shop. 'I hope you get run over by a lorry,' he said to her broad back, and went to the till with the peach nightdress.

Nelly bought Cowboy a camp shirt with eagles on it. He tried it on after their anniversary dinner at home.

'It's gorgeous, Nelly,' he said, standing arms out, like a scarecrow. 'Look. It shows off my tattoo.'

Nelly slid out of her jeans and T-shirt and put on the new nightdress. She smiled up at Cowboy and he could tell she liked it. He swooped her up to his chest and kissed her on the lips, his tongue pressing through her teeth.

'Get away out of that! I taste like chicken,' Nelly said, trying to climb from his arms.

'You taste like love, Nelly.'

The doorbell rang and they looked at each other.

'Who could that be?' Nelly said, looking at the clothes she had tossed on the lino.

'I'll answer it,' Cowboy said, and when he set her down, she yanked the nightdress over her head.

Maureen walked past Cowboy into the hall; he caught the lavender smell of her that always reminded him of baby sick. 'Hello. Come in,' he said.

'Where's Helen?'

Cowboy pointed to the kitchen and he watched her push open the door; Nelly was pulling on her jeans.

'Oh,' Maureen said, 'a bad time, is it?'

'Not really,' said Nelly.

'I'll have a cup of tea so.'

Cowboy slipped into the bedroom and turned on the portable. He could hear Maureen's voice above the TV. She reminded him of people who spoke in foreign languages: no matter what they said, they sounded angry and argumentative. Maureen usually *was* giving out about something and she always needed a witness for whatever was annoying her. Lately, Nelly was that witness.

'I wouldn't mind only Liam is perfect in every other way, Helen. Perfect.'

'Yes,' said Nelly. 'Please God, it will happen though.'

'I told you it won't,' Maureen said. 'Aren't we years trying?'

Cowboy turned up the TV and settled back against the headboard. After a while he fell into a half-sleep where the

TV noise and the two women's voices blended and hummed around his head. When he woke, Maureen was sitting on the edge of the bed.

'What the fuck?' Cowboy said, looking around for Nelly.

Maureen lifted one finger to her lips and placed her other hand on Cowboy's crotch. He stared at her, then plucked her hand off him.

'Think about it,' she said, getting up.

Thirteen months after Cowboy met Nelly, she asked him to sleep with her sister.

'What are you talking about, babe?' Cowboy stared at his wife across the kitchen table and tried to find the hint of a joke around her eyes.

'She wants a baby, Cowboy, and Liam can't give her one.'

'They can adopt.'

'No, they're too old for that; they left it too long.'

'Nelly, you can't be serious. I *hate* Maureen. Jesus, I love *you*. This is fucking mad; I can't even believe we're talking about it.'

'Please, Cowboy. Do it for me.'

'I don't want to, Nell. Don't ask me, please?' He took her hand and tried to look at her, but she kept her eyes low. 'We said no kids. I don't want kids.'

'It'd be *their* kid. Not yours.'

'But you like Maureen about as much as I do. I don't understand why you're asking me to do this.'

'I *owe* her,' Nelly snapped. 'After Mammy and Daddy died she minded me. She reared me. I owe her.'

'I can't do it, Nelly. I just can't.' Cowboy got up from the table and left the house.

At The Cova, he sat and drank alone. He had thought of theirs as a honeymoon marriage: the kissing and hand-holding and talk had never stopped. His love for Nelly was bigger than himself and the same feelings had flowed back to him from her. He thought they were set, secure, perfect.

Sixteen months after Cowboy met Nelly, they were barely speaking. Nelly shut herself down against him and Cowboy felt cold and helpless around her. He came in from work each day to find her eyes locked to the TV; or she would be tucked up in bed, lost in long, deep sleeps.

He sat on the side of their bed one evening and said, 'I'll do it.' Before Nelly could speak, he held up his hand. 'Once, and once only. And if it doesn't work, we'll say no more about it.'

A year and a half after Cowboy met Nelly, he lay over her sister in a B&B on Gardiner Street, eyes closed, gathering his rhythm. The candle Maureen had lit made shadows flick along the walls and Cowboy followed them with his eyes while he jutted and panted. Maureen was still and silent, her fingers pinching the cheeks of Cowboy's bum, her lips turned away from his mouth.

When it was over, she crooked her legs over his hips.

'Don't move for half an hour,' she said, and fell asleep.

Cowboy felt his cock's wet retreat between his legs and he prayed that she would not get pregnant. The queasy heat from the candle made him feel sicker than he already felt.

Maureen woke up and stared at him.

'You can't stand me,' she said.

Cowboy sighed. 'Well, we never really hit it off, did we?'

'No, not really.' She pulled her legs away and lay on her back. 'Helen's lucky to have you,' she said. 'Go on home to her.'

That night, Cowboy held Nelly's back against his

stomach and felt small sobs careening through her body. He put his face into her hair and kissed her neck.

Three weeks later Maureen rang to say the test was negative. 'Thanks for helping me, Nelly,' Maureen said, 'it means a lot.'

Two years after Nelly met Cowboy, she had his name tattooed on the white skin of her inner wrist. She could tell that he liked the tattoo when she showed it to him in The Cova that night; his face rumpled into a crying smile and he kissed her full on the mouth, in front of everyone.

'It's not even my real name,' he said.

Nelly stretched her wrist and looked at the tattoo. 'I know that. What is your real name?'

Cowboy sipped his beer. 'Paris.'

'And who calls you Paris?'

'No one. No one at all.'

BEFORE LOSING THE VALISE, BUT MOSTLY AFTER

M Y FLACCID MOOD had lasted the thirty or so years I had been alive; I was weary and without confidence. But Ernest came into my world and he saw inside me— into my reserves—and with his loving interest, my energies burbled. He was a darling man; with Ernest, I lived. That's how it was, even for a time after I lost the valise. Though his heart shifted away from me then and could not quite settle back.

Peeling away the onion skins of years between that time and now, I can still weep. I see that young me—trying to do a good thing—lugging two valises to the Gare de Lyons. I was excited about taking the Paris-Lausanne Express to join Ernest in Switzerland, where he was reporting for the *Toronto Star*.

❧

A red-jacketed porter hustles up to me and takes my luggage; he is wiry, efficient. He chases me down the platform, his trolley at my ankles. The carriage is muggy and, in the porter's hurry to get me seated, I haven't bought anything to drink or read. He shoves the larger valise onto the top rack and places the other lower down, within my reach.

'*Merci, Monsieur.*'

'*De rien, Madame, de rien,*' he says, and I palm him some coins.

The train won't move for a half hour; I don't have time for a meal in Le Train Bleu café, but I trip back up the platform to a kiosk. The smoke and din of the station starts a push of anticipation in my chest and I smile. How happy Ernest will be to see his girl again. How delighted he'll be that I have carried all of his stories to him, ripe for improvement. We will sit together in the evenings in our hotel room and he'll edit the pages, and I'll drink wine and watch him. Before we eat dinner together. Before we undress to our skins, cuddle into clean sheets and make love, and he whispers, 'Hash, oh my Hash' into my hair.

I buy a bottle of Evian and the *New York Herald*, hoping for news from our far-away home and, maybe, some Parisian gossip. The train puffs and I skitter back to my carriage. A couple have taken the seats opposite mine.

'Good afternoon,' the woman says.

Her husband nods, then grabs at my fingers. 'Walter and Ena Proud,' he says, shaking my hand like he wants to get rid of it.

'Hadley Hemingway,' I say. 'People call me Hash.'

'That's so pretty,' Mrs Proud says. 'Isn't that a pretty name, Walter?'

Like me, they are travelling to Lausanne; Mr Proud knows Ernest—he writes for a paper too.

I settle in and wait for the train to leave; I sip the mineral water and dreg up my dream from last night. I dreamt of starlings: dark swoops of them tangling the sky like a fishing net, then perching in trees, talking to each other as if they were people. In the dream I understood everything they said, but I can't recall any of it now; I try to re-form the starlings' words, but they slip past me like salmon rushing a current. I remember that Ernest told me one time about a man who released a flock of starlings in Central Park, because he thought that North America should contain all the birds mentioned in Shakespeare's plays; Ernest said starlings appear in *Henry IV*. Somehow these tidbits of his always lodge in my head.

Unfolding my newspaper, I glance up to where the porter left my luggage. My throat tightens and I look out the window into the cavern of the station; I dare not believe the empty space on the rack. The big valise is there, but the small one is gone—the one with Ernest's story manuscripts. Staring at my newspaper, I read the headline but it will not make sense; I turn to the Prouds.

'Excuse me. Did you move my luggage?'

Mr Proud shakes his head.

'Is something missing, Mrs Hemingway?' asks Ena Proud, leaning forward and tipping her gloved fingers off my knees; I am shaking and tears scald my eyes.

'The small valise is gone,' I say, in a croak.

'My wife will lend you some of her things. Won't you, darling?'

Mrs Proud nods and smiles gently; a pin-curl falls over one eye and her husband lifts it and tucks it behind her ear. My crying soon becomes like a hysteric's; tears drop fatly from my eyes and I cannot speak without sucking shallow breaths. I spot the conductor near the back of the carriage and flap my hand at him.

'My luggage has been stolen.' I hiccup the words and the conductor sighs.

'Fetch a *gendarme*, man,' Mr Proud barks, and the conductor leaves.

I cannot stop shaking and Mrs Proud makes me swallow brandy from a cup; I try to explain to her about the manuscripts.

'It's all in there. All of it. His notebooks, the typescripts of his stories, the carbons. All of it is in the valise.' When the words topple out of me like that, I fully realise what has happened. 'What will Ernest do?' I say, grabbing at Ena Proud's hand.

'Hush now, Mrs Hemingway. The police will find your suitcase; it can't have gone far,' she says, dabbing at my face with her handkerchief. It smells like violets — rich and powdery.

I sob all night; I am glad the rumbling train muffles the sound. A woman with a large, Italian face fingers rosary beads, prays, and stares at me. The Prouds stretch their legs and lean into each other to sleep. All thoughts of being safe again with Ernest, of Christmas and days of skiing, are gone. I can only think how he will feel when I tell him what I have done. What I have stupidly done.

My eyes sting and my bones are weary. The mountains are black monsters on each side of the carriage, the sky pressing down on them. Our train lumbers on and I wish to get to Switzerland and not to arrive at all. Towards dawn my head falls and jerks into a horrible half-sleep. There are no starlings stalking the trees this time; I cannot dream at all.

'Your wife is most upset, Hemingway,' Mr Proud says, handing Ernest my valise.

Ernest knows this already; he has seen my face and what he has found there is reflected in his eyes. I stand in front of him on the platform, my cheeks hot in the cold air.

'Hash? What is it, Hash?' I start to cry again and shake my head; all my words are jammed behind my tongue. Ernest sits me down on a bench while the train whistles and the other passengers bustle past. 'Are you leaving me, Hash? Please say you're not. Have you fallen for someone else? Talk to me. Have you met someone?'

'Oh, how can you say that?' I rattle with sobs and push

my face into his wool sweater; I swallow my tears. 'It was supposed to be lovely, Ernest. I wanted to surprise you.'

He holds me to him, then away from him. 'Go on.'

'I put everything in: the stories, the poems, your notes. I thought you could work on them, see? While we were here. I thought you could improve everything and that would surely help you get things published.' I gulp a fast breath. 'I put it all in.'

'In where, darling?' His concern has shifted from me to himself; I see it in the pull of his face.

'The small valise.' I look away from Ernest. 'And it was stolen.'

He holds his palms out in front of him and pushes them down, as if he is flattening dough to make bread.

'When you say you "put everything in", Hash, what do you mean exactly?'

'I mean everything,' I whisper. 'The scripts, the carbons, the notebooks.'

Ernest jumps up and walks to the edge of the platform; he groans from deep in his stomach and holds his head in his hands; his fingers press into his temples in a way that must hurt. He looks over at me.

'It's all right, darling. Don't worry,' he says, 'don't worry.' It is a mumbling rant, designed to soothe his own ears. 'We'll get them back.' He hugs me and my tears drop again.

'I'm sorry, Ernest. I'm so sorry.'

It was many years, and three further wives, before Ernest wrote about what had happened. He said that he still missed the stories in the valise. He said he missed them as though they were a blend of his home, his job, his only gun, his small savings. And me.

THE WOMAN IN THE WAVES

I STARE AT *The Woman in the Waves*—on a postcard bought from a bookshop by the river—and imagine, for the thousandth time, that Bea's breasts are like the woman's. I do this before she arrives at my flat, positing all that swollen-upward, otherworldly, blue-tinged flesh onto the not-so-bad breasts that are Bea's.

Bea's key in my front door releases something familiar inside me; a crabby desire. I listen to her walk across the sitting room carpet.

'In here,' I shout, and in a moment she is standing in my bedroom doorway.

'Hello,' she says, and unbelts her coat. 'There's a weird smell in here.'

'As per,' I say, and Bea frowns. 'Come here to me.' I throw back the quilt and she starts to undress while she crosses the floor.

Bea wears her determined face when we make love—she seems to be both here and not here. She concentrates to get to where she wants to be: on her movements, on whatever is in her head, on how she feels. I am an extension.

I close my eyes, lift and kiss her breasts, and she moves over me. Feeling their slight weight, I imagine them heavier; I pull with my lips at her nipples. For me, she is the woman in the waves; her breasts two whelk shells made soft, her underarms a dark, hair-allowed place. I listen to the whoosh of her breath and imagine the sheets as water.

We glide and push through all the yielding and hard

places, and I wonder what it would be like to really do this in the sea—a cold, east-Atlantic romp, our salt mixing with the sea salt; Bea with her arms arched over her head, cheeks red, and white horses lapping her belly, like the woman on the postcard.

'What?' she says, stopping.

'Hmm?' I open my eyes to Bea's fierce, irritated face.

'What about the sea?'

I stare up at her. 'Did I speak?'

'You said "the sea, the sea" or something. Isn't that the name of a film?'

Bea pushes her hair out of her eyes and leans on my chest. Once she is distracted from her build-up, it's hopeless; I feel my cock deadening inside her. She pulls herself off me, making a loud suck, and flumps beside me on the bed.

'Bea—' I reach over.

'Don't,' she says, shoving my hand away. 'The fucking sea. What next?'

I know better than to try to answer her.

There have been times when I've regretted my distracted cupidity. Well, not regretted exactly, maybe more lamented it. Even in the middle of a greedy fantasy about a waitress or a girl on a train, I wonder why I'm doing it. Bea has always seen it—she can pick the girl I'll watch before I do.

I felt, soon after Bea and I had gotten together, that she had taught me to yearn less but, no, I'm as roving-eyed as ever. And that, I suppose, is why she's leaving me.

'Nothing's ever enough for you,' she says. 'I could put my eyes out on sticks.'

'It's because I'm sensitive.'

'No, Georgie, it's actually because you're a selfish prick.'

Bea cries inflated tears and drags her bags to the door; I don't offer to help. Now I have to go through the tedious business of being annoyed with Bea for a while, and of finding someone new.

The girl lets an eggy sneeze and then another; I'm pulled out of a doze by the sneezing and I turn to look at her.

'Sorry,' she says, mopping at the snot with a slice of loo roll.

I fumble in my head for her name; my throat is clotted with night-old wine and my brain swings in its cave, *tharump tharump tharump*. I want to be on my own; I resent this girl's hot limbs beside me. What the fuck is her name? Caitríona? Caitlín? It begins with a C, that much I know. Ciara?

'Dairíne!' I squeak, feeling triumphant.

'Yes, George?'

'What about that swim?' I say.

'Pardon?'

'I said, "What about that swim?"' I form the words slowly, staring at her.

Dairíne is one of those shy girls who takes anything you throw; it makes me want to be mean. She has that predictable Irish beauty: she's dark-haired and blue-eyed, like a TV presenter. Nothing saves her—no dimple, or skewed eye, or manic laugh; she's depressingly gorgeous.

'Did I agree to go swimming last night?' She laughs. 'What was I on?'

'About a gallon of red wine.'

She leaps onto my chest, scaring me a bit. 'I will, so. I'll go with you; I wouldn't want you to think I'm a liar.'

'OK,' I say, wondering what I'm doing.

I've chosen Dairíne's coastal hometown because of a

family holiday when I was ten years old. The woman from the B&B we stayed in sent us a card the Christmas after our stay. As a child, that struck me as a kind act, a singling out of our family as one that mattered. It didn't occur to me that she was touting for the next summer's business. Either way, I was drawn back to Spiddal and its necklace of bungalows overlooking the grey Atlantic.

The beach is a stinking strip of lumpy sand, mostly covered in wrack and kelp. We strip in the shelter of the pier and plunge into the cold water, hand in hand. I swim away from Dairíne, trying to get some heat into my body. She gets back out of the water, yelping. I swim up and down for a bit, then I crawl back to where she sits, in her underwear, on a rock.

'I'm not sure about this now,' she says, 'it's freezing.'

I hold my arms up to her and smile. 'Come on. For me.'

She slides into the water and I hug her; we kiss and our teeth chatter. Dairíne lies against me, cooing and wiggling, and I have to hold onto her waist to keep her from floating away. The smell of cold rock and weed is in the water with us, and I curse the B&B woman for sending that card all those Christmases ago.

Dairíne clings to me, and I look out to sea over her shoulder, at the low humps of the islands. We bob up and down to get warm. I thumb her bra straps off her shoulders, close my eyes and kiss her, pretending that she is Bea. Bea of the arseways smile; Bea of the freckles and flat hair; Bea who is more than good enough for a fool like me. But Dairíne's full tongue and instant moaning throw me off.

'Can you stop that?' I ask.

'What did you say?'

'Stop making that noise; it annoys me.'

Dairíne looks at me, her perfect face pulled sideways;

she drops her arms from around my neck, leans in, and spits between my eyes.

I laugh — a short, shocked gasp — and dunk underwater to clean my face; when I re-emerge, I watch her climb from the sea and pull on her clothes. Well done, girl, I think. And I start the short swim to shore.

AS I LOOK

THE PERVERSE NATURE of some of the art in here annoys me. It's not that I'm anti-flesh—I love bare skin —but some of the nudes in this gallery are deliberately ugly. Take this one with the distended bum. Why did he (it's always a 'he') do that to her? It looks like half of her innards have become her outtards. There's no way the artist knew a woman with a bum like that, I just don't believe it.

I read a slogan once that went something like: 'Do women have to be naked to get into this gallery?'. Around here, the answer might be yes. Naked and nude are two different things, you know. Naked means unprotected or bare, stripped or destitute. Nude means unclothed, or being without the usual coverings. Think about it. There are a lot of nude ladies in this gallery, but are they really *naked*? I mean, are they actually naked, as opposed to nude? Being nude is a beautiful thing (supposedly), but to be naked is to be exposed. I said this to Cam but he said, 'Shut your face and give your arse a chance', which sounds rude, but you'd have to know him. He says things like that.

I don't look especially beautiful with no clothes on; I have a wodgy belly and I'm not pretty, but because I'm tall and a tadge overweight, I have shape; I look like a woman. That makes me happier than you could know. It makes Cam happy too—he likes to ponder my curves. I have friends (women) who have no boobs or hips, and they look as flat and boring as a Dutch landscape; I feel sorry for them.

NUDE

The smells in this gallery—like most—are intoxicating: fresh paint, cedarwoody aftershave, washing powder, hot skin. Galleries turn me on—they are the perfect environment for tension of a sexual nature to erupt between lovers. Cam and I go to a gallery any time we need a little pep and then we run home and devour each other, good and proper. While we make love, I imagine one of the marble statue men coming to life—Bacchus, for instance, with his grapey hair—and Cam thinks of one of those glow-skinned, reclining nudes. His nude throws off her shy shackles and opens herself to him. We can talk about these things because we are that little bit *avant garde*.

We have come to the gallery today as part of The Art Experiment; we are tricky-tricksters, let loose on unsuspecting art lovers. We're going to enjoy this, oh yes we are. Cam and I are a team—just like in life—and his job is to watch my back in case any of the punters 'get physical', as Rodi puts it. Rodi's the organiser of The Art Experiment and she is striking to look at: very blonde and poised.

All the paintings we use have to be famous, that's the deal. Our first painting is *Pisces* by Man Ray, though I've always preferred its French title: *La Femme et son Poisson*. The woman and her fish are equals in the French version, just as they are in the painting, being the same size.

And so we begin.

I stand in front of *Pisces* and glance at the man beside me. He seems a perfect Art Experimentee: older, conservative, with maybe a renegade's heart pumping his blood.

'It's great, isn't it?' I say.

The man rocks his body. 'Mmmn.'

'Man Ray was a bit of a genius.'

'He was certainly versatile,' says The Man.

'I think this painting would look better over there, beside that one, don't you?' I point at de Chirico's *The Uncertainty of the Poet*—a portrait of a female bust with a bunch of bananas.

'Maybe. But I'm sure the curators placed it here for a reason.'

The Man is about to walk away, so I pull *Pisces* from the wall. (It's a replica, of course, I should state that, in case anyone is getting antsy.)

'Here, hold this,' I say. 'I'm going to put them together. See if I'm right.'

The Man steps back from me and looks around him. Cam is hovering nearby (my protector!) but there's no one else in this part of the gallery. I shove the Man Ray into The Man's hands and walk over to the de Chirico.

'Fuck,' says The Man, looking from Cam to me. 'Hey, you're not allowed to do this.'

It surprises me that he uses the F word so readily—he doesn't look the type.

'You're helping me,' I say. 'I want to see them together.'

The Man looks all around him again; he goes to lean the painting against the wall and dash off, but doesn't. I take the (pretend) Dali that hangs next to *The Uncertainty of the Poet* off the wall and walk back towards him. Cam has disappeared all of a sudden and that makes my throat tighten.

'Miss, this is not right. It's unlawful. You'll get into trouble,' The Man says.

'Take this.' I grab *Pisces* and shove the Dali into his hands.

'Miss, I . . .'

Where the hell is Cam gone? Why has he upped and left me here with this old geezer, who could be a rapist? I hang the Man Ray beside the de Chirico and draw a quick, fizzing breath. Well, what do you know? They look bloody perfect together. Super. The blue sky above the bust in *Poet* is a mirror of the curve of water under the fish in *Pisces*; the two nudes twist coyly away from one another; the mad combi of the bananas and the fish seems somehow to fit: it's all sensuality and food and phallic-ness. The symmetry is uncanny and I suddenly understand that both paintings are about sex.

'Amazing,' The Man says, turning to smile at me. 'You were right.'

'You're my accomplice now,' I say.

The Man puts one arm around me and we stand gazing at the paintings. I can feel the heat of his hand on my waist; between my legs begins to swell. My face lifts to his—all on its own it feels like—and his face leans down to mine. We kiss: his tongue is luscious, firm. He pulls away and smiles again.

'I'm surprised the alarms didn't go off,' The Man says.

'We'd better go.'

'Surrealism is all about the hidden self,' The Man whispers, as we rush hand in hand through the connecting rooms to the exit. 'It's about obsession.'

'I know.'

We pass a girl who drops a metallic stone on the floor; another girl flicking a yo-yo; a girl wearing red velour pumps; a girl with a pink scarf tied around her waist. We pass Cam, his long front flush to Rodi's front; his hands tangled into her hair and his lips hovering over her head.

We make the front door before they see us, The Man and me, the faux Dali still in his fist.

JACKSON AND JERUSALEM

SHE TOLD ME on the phone that her gaff was called Jerusalem. This was before I knew who she was, or anything about her, and I thought it was an awful weird name to call a place. But famous people are always doing that sort of thing, like calling their kids Banana or Tuesday and nobody bats an eye. Her gaff was easy to find — the walls were painted a mad orange — but it was still a typical auld dear's place, with the windows cluttered up with Saint Anthony and the Child of Prague and swaggy curtains. Her voice was real posh, but I knew it would be, because Christopher talked like that and he was her nephew and my teacher. I hate yapping on the phone, so I said I'd call round, and she could have a look at me.

I stood in her doorway, smelling the hall's beer-and-onion stink. Her hair was dyed off her head — black as a crow's wing — and she was wearing a manky apron, covered in paint splotches. She didn't look at me like I was a scumbag. Behind her was a table with twenty different statues of the Blessed Virgin toppling over each other.

'Christopher never said you were real holy,' I said.

'I'm not. Not on your fucking Nelly.' She picked up a Mary, who was holding a nudie Jesus, and petted it. 'I like their colours and their forms.' She put down the statue and stuck out her hand. 'Magda Bolding. I take it you're Jackie?'

'Not on *your* fucking Nelly,' I said, doing a snobby accent like hers, and making the — ing in 'fucking' ting around inside my mouth like a pinball through Sharkey's Shootout. 'The name's Jackson.'

Magda grinned. 'OK, Jackson. I think Christopher was right: you and I are going to get along.' She slammed the front door and flapped me through the hall to the kitchen, like I was an escaped hen. 'Let's have a goo at you.'

Leaning against her sink, I twitched at the ends of my hoodie, while Magda looked me up and down. I felt a bit thick in my new combats: they were too baggy, too camouflagey, too everything. She squinced up her eyes.

'What?' I said.

She took my face in her hands and tilted my head; her fingers were cool and soft, like a doctor's.

'Great cheek bones. Any girl would kill for them. Clear blue eyes. Good, good. Remove the hat.' I pulled off my beanie. 'Wow,' she said, 'hair like a Botticelli cherub.'

'Gimme that.' I grabbed the hat and shoved it back on.

'Why have those beautiful curls if you're going to hide them, boy?'

I shrugged. 'Don't want to look like all the other fellas.'

'Ah, a maverick. Perfect.' She put her hands on my shoulders and looked into my eyes; I stared back. Somewhere in her face there was a smile but it didn't curve through her lips. 'To the studio,' she said, twisting me around to face the back door.

Her studio was a massive shed in the garden; it smelt sweet inside, like a furniture shop, and it was warm. Magda told me to sit and she clipped paper to an easel. I wiggled in the seat, stretching my legs, and pulling my hands in and out of my lap. She stood, in her dirty apron, as though she was straddling an invisible horse; her hair flopped over her shoulder like a mane. I was mortified, her eyes kept landing on me; I fidgeted and looked at the floor, the walls, the ceiling. I wondered why snobs always wore such hickey clothes, like they couldn't afford proper stuff.

66

'Keep still, Jackson. Please.'

Her pencil scratched across the page and she looked at me, then back at the sketch; I was getting bored.

'A masterpiece, Magda, is it?' I said.

'You betcha.'

Flick-flick with her eyes; scratch-scratch with the pencil. My body wouldn't calm down; I wanted to chill, let my thoughts go blank, like I do in school, but it wouldn't happen. I looked around at the paintings that were hung on the walls. They were the kind of things Christopher brings our class to look at in art galleries in town; they looked like a mentler had done them. But some of them were OK—you could see people and buildings in the jumble of paint. There were a few paintings where nobody had any clothes on; I stared at them, then turned away, but my eyes were dragged back again. The canvases were lumpy with paint, but the people's skin—the women's boobs and all—looked soft and alive. I wondered how Magda had done that.

She was watching me. I eyeballed her. 'You needn't think I'm going to strip,' I said.

Magda frowned and sucked her pencil; I knew the soggy wooden taste it'd leave on her tongue, the paint chips that'd stick to her teeth. I wanted to take it out of her mouth.

'What exactly did Christopher tell you about coming here, Jackson?'

'That you were doing some big, important painting and you needed a young fella to model. That you'd pay me.'

'Did he mention nudity at all?'

I scuffed the floor with my runner. 'No.'

'So, he didn't explain the tableau I'm working on?' I shook my head and she sighed. 'My nephew is lackadaisical in everything he does, says and is.'

'Is that the same as "laxadaisy"? That's what my Da calls me.' I snorted. 'Well, one of the things.'

'Yes, the very same.' Magda pulled over a chair and sat; she kept her mouth open, and I could see spit bubbles like spills of milk on her tongue. Normally that kind of stuff makes me feel sick, you know, other people's gobs and ear-wax and snot and stuff. But, even though she was an auld dear, there was—and is—something fresh about Magda, something kinda pure. 'Do you know your Bible, Jackson?' she said.

I jumped up. 'I fucken knew you were a Holy Joe.'

'Sit.' I sat. 'I already told you that's not the case; listen to me for a minute.'

She took my hands; I hate anyone touching my skin, but I let her hold on to me, if that was what she wanted.

'Go for it,' I said.

'In Saint Luke's Gospel it says that Jesus went to cele-brate the Passover in Jerusalem every year with his parents. But, when he was twelve, instead of returning to Nazareth with Mary and Joseph, he stayed behind. On the way home, they realised he was missing and it took them days to find him; he was in a temple in Jerusalem. Of course, they'd been frantic, and they were annoyed with him but, when Mary gave out, Jesus said: "Why were you so worried? Did-n't you know I'd be in my Father's house?"'

'So?'

'So, I love the idea of Jesus as blasé teenager and divin-ity in one.' Magda smiled.

'Div-what?'

'Divinity. A divine being. A God. Anyway, this tableau I'm painting is of Jesus in the temple, talking to the priests. But, I want to represent Jesus naked, to show his power but, at the same time, his innocence.'

'Jesus in the nude? With priests? He'd better watch out.'
I laughed but Magda didn't; she squeezed my hands and
made a question with her eyes. 'If I do it,' I said, 'you're not
to let on. Not even to Christopher. If that gock tells the
other teachers, next thing it'll be all over the school, and I
might as well kill myself.'

Magda tossed her hair back and laughed; I could see her
fillings like a pile of black full stops along her teeth. She
brought my hands to her mouth, kissed my fingers, and
said, 'Thank you'.

The first morning of posing started kind of poxy; Magda
was narked with me because I came late to Jerusalem. I'd
had a fight with my auld fella and slept half the night on a
street bench, freezing my nuts off. I spent the morning in
Abrakebabra, drinking tea to warm up.

'It's half past ten,' she said, blocking the way into her
house.

'Yeah?'

'If you plan to be a smart bollocks, Jackson, you can shag
off now.'

'Language, Magda.' I grinned.

'Go!' she shouted, and I knew she was real pissed off, so
I stopped acting the maggot, and said I'd never be late
again. A day with her had to be miles better than going
home to my Da and *his* nutsy mood. She blinked, then
stepped back to let me in.

I got used to being in the nip. I mean, I hated it at first
and I was totally scarlet, but Magda didn't care whether you
were in clothes or out of them.

'Artists are like doctors, where the human body is concerned,' she said. 'Bare flesh is just part of the working day.'

Still, I undressed behind a screen, then peeped around,

and she called me out with one crooked finger; I shuffled into the middle of the room with my hands over my bits. Magda put me standing where she wanted me and pulled my arms to my sides; I felt a jump in my balls but then everything settled.

'Now, Jackson, pretend I'm not here. Think about something else, put your mind in another zone,' she said, going to her easel. 'Relax.'

The problem is, when someone tells me to relax, I coil real tight. When a nurse or someone like that says to take deep breaths, I start choking and my mind jumps from seizures, to bleeding to death, to my funeral. But it was going to be a long day and I needed the money; and I wanted to do things right for Magda. I forced myself to hang looser and slow down my thinking. After a while, I went into some numb, faraway place where I couldn't feel my skin or bones as part of myself anymore. And it felt good.

My Da said I made him sick. He had the light on and he stood over my bed, calling me a queer-boy and a lezzie-lover. I squinted at him, half-in-half-out of a dream where I was riding a Harley across America, all free and easy; I wanted to deck him for taking me out of there.

'Stripping off at the drop of a hat. You're a homo, Jackie, I always knew it.' He was minging of drink, falling round the place, and waggling a fist at me. He'd heard about the painting; I don't know how, but he had. 'You're a weirdo. Like all the fucken Noonans.'

'Shut up about the Noonans.' I hated when he slagged my Ma's family.

'*Shut up about the Noonans.*' He copied my voice, squeaking it through his teeth. 'All those Noonans are too big for their boots and them with not a pot to piss in. And that includes your precious Ma.' He stood there with spits hanging from his mouth, his face beetroot. 'Where's your lovely Ma now, Jackie, what? Fucked off with herself, didn't she?' He whacked my leg through the quilt and shouted. '*Didn't she?*'

'You're bleeding mad.' I jumped out of bed and tried to get past him.

'Come back here, you,' he roared. He caught my hair, dragged me down and shoved my face into the bed. 'Makin' a fucken fool of me, you bastard.' He pinched his fingers into my neck and pushed my face into the quilt. 'Dancin' round in your pelt so some hippy-bitch can get her jollies. Have you lost the plot?'

I could hardly breathe but I reefed away from him and fell backwards; I hopped up.

'You're a cunt, Da, and no one likes you. Not your drinking buddies, not my Ma, not me. Not *anyone*.'

I pucked him hard and he toppled; his arms waved like someone falling off a building. His arse hit the carpet with a flump. Next thing he bends forward and starts to bawl; I stood over him, watching snot bubble from his nose and tears fall onto his chest. I put my hand out but he smacked it away; he was blubbing like an overgrown baby. I'm fucked if I didn't feel sorry for him.

'Da? Jaysus, Da, come on.'

'Get out, Jackie,' he sobbed, 'get out. I'm ashamed to call you my son.'

The painting was getting there. Every one of the priests was really Christopher in a different pose: him with a beard, him with long hair, him with a hat or a turban. Your average person wouldn't notice that it was all the one man, but I knew, and I liked knowing.

Magda did different versions of me too: back views, side views, full-frontals. They were deadly—I looked like me, but not like myself, if you know what I mean. I was real proud of the painting and it was a good buzz, being at Magda's, eating her weird cheese and stuff, and drinking coffee and yapping.

'OK, Jackson, I'm ready to put Jesus in; I need to find the perfect pose,' she said, one morning, and asked me to help her choose it. We lined up her oil sketches.

'This sideways one is good, you can see my face,' I said. She shook her head. 'What about from the back?'

'No. The exact opposite, I think.' Magda chawed her paintbrush and I pulled it from her mouth.

'You'll wreck your teeth.'

She ruffed my hair and smiled; her hand landed on my shoulder. She lifted my hair and looked at my neck. The bruises from my Da were still there, like a tattooed necklace of finger-shaped beads. Magda looked at me.

'Do you want to tell me anything?'

I shook my head. 'It's just my Da,' I said.

She put her arm around me and hugged me into her side and, with her skin light on my skin, we chose the best position for Jesus in the temple.

How was I supposed to know that Magda Bolding was famous? I'd never heard of her. And by the state of her clothes and gaff, I'd never have guessed either. Christopher didn't say his auntie was Mrs Modern Irish Art, but he never said much, in fairness. At school, he'd go into his cubby in the art room to smoke, while we painted still-lifes of rotten apples. And how was I to know, either, that Magda's *Jesus in the Temple* would end up on the telly, bonging out the Angelus, with my micky hanging out for all the world to gawk at?

As for my Da, well, he thought it was great gas.

'Here, Jesus,' he'd squawk, 'turn that water into wine, like a good man'.

'You fucken wish,' I'd say, and he'd ball his fist at me.

'Wine is piss,' he'd say then, and, 'I suppose you're off to Jerusalem today'. Ha-ha-ha.

The night Magda and me went on *The Late Late Show*, he made all his buddies in Maguire's watch it. Mr Maguire told me my Da went mad if anyone clinked a glass while Pat Kenny was yakking to Magda and me about the making of the painting. My Da would never have told me himself that he even watched it, never mind making his pals watch. We were still sparring, but Da was a bit wary of me. I might've thought it was a kind of respect because I was doing something new, something he wouldn't have had the balls to do, but he was still the same mouthy, antsy arsehole. Everything was all fun and laughs until he decided it wasn't again.

Anyway, whether I knew Magda was mad famous or not, I still think I would have posed for her. She's a bit of a hippy —I knew that the minute I saw her—but she's the kind of auld bird who makes you feel like the most special person in the world when you're with her. That's one of the real gifts she has: making everyone feel important; as important as herself.

XAVIER

Y OU ARRIVED IN BARCELONA with no plan other than to experience it. In your head it was a gothic place, all teetering Gaudiesque towers and endless nights. The reality of it wasn't too different: the maze of laneways off the Ramblas pumped their dark sensuality like a medieval carnival, night and day, and there was a vibrancy to the roaming crowds of rich and poor. Barcelona didn't wear the pristine frilliness of Germanic cities, it had its own dirty-sweet, lived-in charm, like a treasured vintage dress. The Gaudi buildings weren't everywhere, like you had expected, but the place was beautiful and unlike any other you'd been in. Arriving in October, you found the city still basking under summer's heat and you were glad of it, after a rainy Dublin September.

The studio you rented was in El Raval, overlooking a busy laneway that was chock-a-block with cheap Indian restaurants. It took two months for you to adjust your body to the rhythms of the neighbourhood: quiet mornings, noisy nights. The women in the flat opposite—there were five of them and two small babies—were performers, seamstresses or prostitutes: spangled, sequiny costumes lounged on rows of wall hooks, or sat in their laps for mending. You could lie in your bed by the window and look across the alley, through the railings of the balcony, into their flat. They may have been Cuban: they shimmied and shuffled together every afternoon to Latino music, swinging the children in their arms occasionally and shouting at each other constantly.

XAVIER

Five days a week you pulped fruit and vegetables into long glasses for thirsty tourists. Seven nights a week you played with your new friends: a gaggle of Aussies, Catalans and Brits, with the odd Kiwi thrown into the mix for flavour. Xavier—beautiful, angry Xavier—was a native. You met him, ridiculously, in an Irish bar called The Ramblers. Like most Irish abroad, you flocked to the Guinness sign when it presented itself in your first week in the city. The workers in the bar were all English, the beer was twice the price of everywhere else, but the music was from home and it was comforting, some nights, to hear familiar accents.

You had spotted Xavier early on in the evening; he didn't look like any other Catalans you'd met. He was scruffy: he wore a raggy T-shirt, his head was dirty with stubble and he looked belligerent and unhappy. But he was watching you, just as you couldn't stop watching him. Chatting with your workmates, you flicked your eyes in his direction from time to time and he stared back. It was late when he came up behind you at the bar and wound his hand into your hair, like a snake.

'Your hair is like ashes.'

'Is that a compliment?'

'Yes,' he said, but pronounced it *jess*. He asked if you were from Ireland and when you said that you were, he nodded.

'Are you from Barcelona?'

'Near here.'

You leaned your head back off the end of the bed; the balcony door was open to let any small breeze blow through the studio. The ceiling fan was frozen again—it gave off an eerie whine that sounded like cats in heat. With your eyes half-shut, the green ceiling rose seemed to shiver and spin.

Xavier was sucking at your throat, pumping your breasts between his hands and grunting with each thrust he made. Sweat slid from his thighs to yours, from his belly to yours. His long body cleaved onto you in a perfect way. Like he said, you were a fit. Your neck was sore from holding it back over the hard edge of the mattress; you opened your eyes fully. The Latino women were watching you and Xavier: they had gathered on their balcony, and they languished there, staring at your heaving bodies as if they were looking at a film on TV.

You locked your eyes onto the eyes of the eldest woman, the one you had christened Rosa because of her china doll-red cheeks. She fanned her face with a magazine, then raised one eyebrow at you. You smiled, lifted your head and kissed Xavier deeply, forcefully. He said he was going to come and you matched his jutting and urged him on until he collapsed onto you with his familiar whimper. You kissed wetly, for a long time, and when you looked across the alley again, the women were gone.

Xavier rolled a joint for the two of you to share and you sat up in the bed, watching his nimble fingers skin, flame, crumble, roll and light. It would've taken you ten minutes to do it, so you were glad he was rolling and not you. He offered you the first drag and the smoke hit the back of your throat like pepper. You breathed long on its heat again, then handed it to him.

'You know, in Ireland we pronounce your name "Ecks-save-yer".' You giggled. 'Or some people say "Save-yer".'

He snorted, blowing smoke through his nose in ragged puffs. 'Say that again. Ecks-something?'

'Ecks-save-yer. It's terrible, isn't it? *Ecks-save-yer, come in for your dinner, it's gettin' cauld.*' You laughed. 'The way you say it is so much sexier. *Xavier. Xavier.*'

'I like your name too. Lillis. It's pretty. What does it mean?'

'Oh, it's the flower, the lily. It's Greek. My mother has absurd taste—she called my brother Robin, like the bird, and he's this enormous, grizzly thing.'

Xavier pressed his hand into your stomach, rubbing at the mingled sweat that was still gathered there. You loved the look of his honey-brown skin, with its lattice of tattoos, against your body which stubbornly stayed as pale as milk.

'I wish I had a tan,' you said.

'I like your skin,' he fingered your shoulder, 'it's like the inside of a turnip.' Your face must have dropped. 'I mean that in a good way,' he added, smiling, and he kissed your nose. You touched the raised veins on his inner arms; they were as darkly blue as a tracery of rivers on a vellum map.

'You're so gorgeous, Xavier.'

He leaned over and kissed you, long and lovingly. The smoke had made you both sluggish and his tongue felt thick and welcome against yours.

In Café Alex you ate bruise-tipped asparagus spears, pimentos that were both smoky and sweet, and beef tomatoes slick with olive oil. Xavier poked at his dish of tapas with a cocktail stick—every so often stabbing a piece of feta or a glossy green olive—and swigged mightily at a bottle of beer. Night had closed down fast over the city; Xavier looked at his watch, said he had to meet someone about something. He was jittery and, you thought, angry-seeming again but you were afraid to ask who he was meeting and why. You gulped at your wine and talked about the letter your brother had sent, all about the new boy he'd met and how he thought this one was 'the one'.

'As usual,' you said, and smiled, thinking of Robin. A

sudden compassion for him welled out of nowhere and you realised you were missing him a lot. 'Robin's great, you know? We get on well, more like friends than brother and sister; I can really talk to him.' Xavier barely lifted his eyes to show he was listening, so you shut up and concentrated on eating. It was late and this was the first meal you'd had all day.

'Let's go,' he said.

'I'm still eating.'

'Hurry up.'

'I don't want to hurry up, I've loads left.' You pointed at the various tapas dishes ranged around your plate. Xavier stood and hovered over the table clicking his fingers, in an absent, urgent way. In the end, you slugged back your wine and stuffed the last of your food into your mouth; a slew of oil rilled down your chin and you wiped it away as you followed him out onto plaça Reial.

The square was heaving with people: open-air diners, buskers, jugglers, wanderers and tourists. You stopped, looked around and spotted Marina, the small girl from London who often came into the café you worked in, for a chat. You waved, but she looked like she was off her head: her eyes were closed and she was playing a tin whistle; her head lolled and she lurched from table to table, begging for a few pesetas. A huge-armed man with a cluster of dreads at the nape of his neck stayed near her, watching, never letting her stray too far. Looking at him watching Marina made you feel sick. Turning around, you realised that Xavier was gone, lost in the mill of people on the square.

You were a little drunk and you didn't like the idea of having to walk the dim alleyways alone. Running into the middle of the plaça Reial, you hoped to see Xavier ahead of you, but you scanned the crowds and didn't find him. You walked quickly up a narrow street to get to the Ramblas, nearly tripping over two people who were sprawled on the ground in the dark. The night's heat gathered around your face and your upper lip began to dampen; you folded your arms around your body, dipped your head and ploughed through the people who were walking towards you. Then, realising that you probably looked agitated, you slowed your pace and stepped more surely; you were glad to see the lit-up markets stalls of the Ramblas ahead. Hearing someone running behind you, you turned to see Marina coming up the alleyway. She was clutching the tin whistle and her bag of coins; she banged into you and grabbed at your arm.

'Please, please, help me. You know me, you know me,' she babbled. Her eyes were rolling in their sockets and she looked feverish, but her clutching hand was strong on your arm. You told her to calm down and glanced behind to see if her dreadlocked minder was coming after her.

'Marina! Marina! It's me, it's Lillis,' you said, shaking her. She seemed to be asleep on her feet. 'Can you run?' She nodded, her head bobbing like a toddler's, so you dragged her, half-running, up the alley to the Ramblas. Once there, you weaved through people and crossed the road into El Raval, then took a roundabout route to your studio on Carrer de Sant Pau, where you shoved her up the stairs ahead of you.

You woke to a rhythmic pounding on the door. When you opened your eyes, you saw the back of Marina's short dirty-blonde hair beside you on the pillow and couldn't figure out why she wasn't Xavier. The wheening of the ceiling fan blended with the thumping that went on and on. You remembered what had happened.

'Who is it?'

'It's me. Who do you think it is?'

You let Xavier in. 'Where the hell did *you* get to?' He saw Marina on the bed, still dressed in worn ski pants and T-shirt. 'What the fuck is she doing here?'

'She had nowhere to go.'

'Get her out of here, she's a dirty junkie.'

'She's only a kid.'

'Get her *out*! She's a fucking pro,' he shouted.

'Keep your voice down, Xavier. This is my place and I'm letting her stay.'

'Do you have any idea who her pimp is, Lillis?' You shook your head. 'It's French Bernard. Do you know him?'

'I've seen him. Big. Dreadlocks.'

'You don't want to make an enemy of that man, believe me, Lillis. I should know.'

'What could I do? She needed a little help.'

'For your own sake, and mine, get rid of her.' Xavier was pointing his finger into your face. You pushed it away.

'She's staying.'

He let a roar and kicked at the leg of a chair, sending it skidding across the tiles; it crashed into the wall. Marina didn't even stir.

'Lillis, make a choice: if she stays, I go.'

You looked at him, at the raw anger that tensed his whole body. Then you looked at Marina, curled on the bed like a baby.

'I think you'd better leave.'

Xavier threw up his arms. 'You crazy bitch.' He turned away, then swung back, went to say something and stopped himself; he crossed the floor, opened the door and looked at you. 'Thank you, fuck you, and good bye.' The slamming door made you wince.

'Goodbye, Xavier,' you said, to the air. Marina sat up, rubbed at her eyes. You smiled at her. 'How are you doing? Breakfast?'

She stood up out of the bed, reached for her whistle and bag. 'I have to go and find Bernard,' she said, 'he'll be looking for me.'

'Wait Marina.' You put your hand on her shoulder. 'Will you be OK? Will Bernard not be angry with you for running off?'

Marina shrugged. 'Thanks, Lillis. For the bed. See you around, yeah?'

You let her go.

NIGHT FISHING

TWICE A YEAR they come here, to her home-place. He and she. One winter visit, one summer. She is a good daughter, the kind anyone would be glad to have. He is a good son-in-law: helpful, fine-featured, polite — like all French people, they think. He loves nature, the outdoors. The Irish landscape refreshes him, gets him ready for another half-year in the rush and din of Paris.

Sheila, the good daughter, settles into the house, fussing over her parents and acting younger than she is; she enjoys the worn familiarity of home. Henri, the good son-in-law, chops logs and paints rooms; he hefts furniture from B to A and goes for long drives into the mountains, where he likes to walk. His walks take him through places his wife has never been: Lugnaquilla, The Glen of Imaal, Poulaphouca, The Sally Gap.

After long days, he returns to the house, fresh-cheeked and happy, mud dappling his trousers. His parents-in-law and wife turn vague faces from the television to ask him about his adventures. He describes the things he's seen: plump pheasants barking in long grass, burbling streams heavy with fool's gold, and black, bottomless lakes.

'Who'd have thought nature could be such fun?' his wife says, her head pulling back to the TV screen, like a strung puppet.

'Yes, who'd have thought?' Henri says.

Henri likes to fish. His father-in-law gave him a rod last Christmas and since then he's been hooked. Now his trips to the mountains are longer: fishing takes time. He is still learning the best ways to land a catch: he reads about night-fishing and sleepy prey, about how to use bait to full effect. Henri gives a lot of time to his new hobby. Sheila doesn't mind too much—there's a new shopping centre near her parents' home, it's state of the art and it stays open all night.

'State of the art?' Henri says, and she nods. He kisses her nose and packs his tackle into the boot of the hired car. His wife stands in the driveway and riffles through her hand-bag.

'Is it not a bit late to go fishing?' She looks at her watch and pulls a doubtful face. 'I mean, in the summer it's nice and bright, but in December?'

'I know my way around. Besides, this is the best time: the darkness makes the catch dull-headed. I can pounce on them unawares.' Henri kisses her again, on the lips. 'See you later, *chérie*.'

'Don't stay up there too long,' Sheila says, and rummages some more in her bag, then holds up the car keys for him to see. She hops into her mother's car and drives off.

Henri snaps shut the boot door and sits in behind the wheel. He makes a mental note of the contents of the boot: fishing rod, tackle box, bait, knife, rope, wipes, rags, waders and plastic bags. A change of clothes. Everything stowed in its place. He breathes deep on the leatherette smell of the car, smiles to himself, and pulls out of the driveway, humming a tune. Dusk is landing over the city like a silver cloak. It makes Henri happy to watch the sky change from salmon-grey to ink-blue as he drives towards the dark hump of the mountains. He snaps on the headlights and wonders if the night will be a success.

In the pub, three-legged cooking pots, cracked crockery and whiskey jars clutter up shelves and hang from the ceiling. Pearly smoke from the turf fire makes Henri's throat dry; he sips a pint of stout and wiggles his bum on the wooden bench, trying to get comfortable. It's quiet: a spattering of locals and some German tourists—men—are the only others there. Not very hopeful, Henri thinks. The barman is watching football on the television, then he nips out for a cigarette.

'That fucking smoking ban,' he calls out to Henri and the others, when he comes back. 'It's pissing rain and perishing cold out there.' He rubs his hands together.

'It always rains in Ireland, that's what I like about it,' Henri says, and the barman shakes his head and sighs.

The front door swings wide and a girl bustles through. A small backpack makes her look like a tortoise and her hair is dark from the rain. Henri glances at her, then back into the heart of the fire. He holds his hands out to the flames and flexes his fingers; he allows himself a small smile before lifting a paperback from his jacket pocket. He puts on a pair of reading glasses and skims his eyes over the lines of words, until he feels the girl looking at him. Then he lifts his face to her. She smiles and Henri smiles back—a shy, friendly curl of the mouth.

'Mind if I sit down?' she asks. She has the kind of face Henri likes: round and open.

'Be my guest,' he says, waving at the seat beside him and dropping his nose into the book again.

'It's wild out there,' she says, cosying her behind into the fireplace, before sitting down. Henri looks at her.

'Yes,' he says, 'crazy Irish weather.' Antipodean, he thinks. A long way from home.

'You're not from here, are you? What accent is that?' the

girl says, leaning towards him. Big eyes. He looks at her wide, white smile and licks his lips.

'French. I teach languages at a school here in Dublin,' he says.

'Hey, I'm a teacher too. We have something in common already.' She laughs. Henri laughs too and asks if she would like a drink.

Henri flicks the fishing rod back over his shoulder and swings his arms forward. There is no moon and he can't see far, but he hears the neat *splosh* as the line hits the water. He pictures the weight and the hook sinking into the lake, through weeds and spawny stuff and past shoals of fish. He wonders how many water creatures see the fishing line diving down, down; do they nudge at it, taste it, notice the float clung to the water above their heads? He likes to imagine the baited hook's journey into the murk that holds its secrets tight. Henri is hungry; he thinks about food and pulls his feet out of the sucking mud in the shallows and tries to stand more squarely. The waders make him clumsy and his toes are dead with the cold.

The lake is like a blackened window, wide and dark and reflective. Banks of reeds frill its edges and they shush in the breeze; Henri stands as still as he can for a few moments to listen to them—they're whispering to each other. There's ice in the air and it stings his nostrils; he sniffs and holds out one hand, palm up. The rain is back and it has turned to a light hail. Henri listens to it plopping against the water; he thinks he might go home soon, his arms ache and he feels tired. And he's looking forward to a nice sandwich; there'll be slices of beef in the fridge, left-over from dinner time.

It had taken a long time to lash the ropes because his hands were so cold; he'd forgotten his gloves. Stupid. He'd had to leave her for a while too—bobbing in the rushes like an unbasketed Moses—while he went to find rocks to weigh her down. Henri wasn't familiar with this side of the lake, he hadn't known there was no stony beach here. The drink had made him sloppy. He had drank three pints—more than usual—and he'd lost the reading glasses somewhere. Again, stupid. But it had all gone smoothly, really—he had liked easing her out of this world.

'One more,' he'd said, into her ear, when he felt her neck grow lax under his fingers. Her skin was cool and firm-soft, like uncooked pastry.

Henri lets himself into the house, makes a sandwich and eats it in the dark of the kitchen. He has a shower in the downstairs bathroom. The scald of the water clears the smog of his hangover and he scrubs himself hard all over. He brushes his teeth and slooshes mouthwash around his mouth to kill the taste of beer and beef. A burp escapes his throat and he puts his hand to his mouth and excuses himself. He ate too fast. Henri examines his teeth in the mirror, grins at his own reflection and switches out the bathroom light.

When he slips into bed beside Sheila, she turns to face him. She is warm all over, heavy with sleep; her nightdress is rucked over her hips. Henri slips his hand under her nightie, onto the pouch of her belly. In the dim darkness, he can make out the cabbage-rose pattern on the curtains and Sheila's old dolls, lying listless and grim on a shelf, like corpses. He listens to the water pipes gurgling in the attic.

'You were gone a long time,' Sheila murmurs, trying to open her eyes. 'Catch anything?' Henri slides his other arm up her back, hugs her to him. He puts his mouth close to her ear.

'Just one, *chérie*. I threw it back—it wasn't worth keeping.' He kisses her cheek, then along her neck.

'They never are, are they?' she whispers, and lifting his fingers to her mouth, she kisses them, one by one.

ROY LICHTENSTEIN'S *NUDES IN A MIRROR*: WE ARE NOT FAKE!

W<small>E ARE SO GLAD</small> that Roy isn't alive to see what's happened to us because, oh my Lord, he would die.

Yes, we're comic-strippy—not exactly *The Rokeby Venus*—but we are of-our-time, same as old Mrs Rokeby. Whoever she was. And, we are not pleased that some weirdos want to get at us because we are undressed. And that there are fancy-schmanzies who think we're dumb because we were modelled from models. Hullo, that is how it operates, and our models loved their work and were good at it. How many of you can say that?

I am going to speak for both of us—I'm the forefront figure in *Nudes in a Mirror*—so I saw what happened a lot clearer than what's-her-face in the back there. I guess I should begin by saying that we are Americans, so Europe and Austria were all new to us, and I, for one, was nervous about the trip.

But the Bregenz Gallery was a real nice place and the curators took such care hanging us. Our canvas is B-I-G, but they gave us a vast cement wall, prettily spaced from *Female Head* (one of Roy's seventies gals). We were more than pleased, hollering back and over to each other when the gallery was empty.

Boy oh boy, then it all changed.

Saturday afternoon, in strolls a perfectly decent-looking woman, with glasses and boring hair. Let's call her Brigitte. She stands in front of our canvas and I watch her, watching me. Brigitte appreciates our benday dotted skin and my faintly concerned expression as I primp; she acknowledges the artful diagonal slashes that tell her I am looking into a mirror. She is wise enough, I can tell, to appreciate the bubblegum wrapper-ness of Roy's style, and the madcap border of yellow paint that frames us. Brigitte is a discerning woman; she likes a day out at the gallery. All that is missing is a bench for her to park her ass on, so she can study us in comfort.

Brigitte rootles in her purse; maybe my frosted pink lips have reminded her to reapply her gloss. She glances over her shoulder to where Friedrich, the security guard, is slumped in a chair, carving black crescents of dirt from under his nails. Brigitte steps closer to me, clutching her purse in front of her chest, like an external womb.

I am suddenly alert; this kind of furtiveness usually means only one thing: she is going to try to use her camera. Seriously, I don't mind. Most people become giddy in galleries and want snaps for their photo albums, to show their relatives back home how cultural they are; to show themselves the same thing when they are back in their rut. But the Lichtenstein Foundation don't want unauthorised pictures of Roy's pictures here, there and everywhere, if you get me.

Friedrich looks up, rakes his museum-glazed eyes over the patrons, then yawns hugely; he gazes at his fingernails like he's in love. Brigitte holds the zipper of her purse together, looks over at Friedrich, then turns back to face me. OK, here goes; she is feeling in her purse again for the camera, her eyes riveted forward. I see this all the time—

'rigor mortis nonchalance' I call it: people looking tense when they are trying so hard to be casual.

But, oh my Lord, she suddenly leaps towards me and I see a jackknife plunge through the air in four sharp shots: slash, *slash*, slash, *slash*. This Brigitte is purposeful and mean. Friedrich is on her in seconds, grabbing her arms and screeching, '*Nein, nein, nein!*' and a man who was admiring *Female Head*, runs and clutches her by the waist from behind. Brigitte drops the jackknife and her purse.

'*Es ist eine Fälschung!* It is a fake!' she hoots, struggling and writhing, trying to get away.

She scratches Friedrich in the face, and he and the man wrestle her to the floor. Brigitte bites the man in the leg, gnashing like a dog. He screams and pulls her off his shin, but he holds her down.

A female security guard grabs Brigitte's purse and searches it; she pulls out a screwdriver and a can of red spray paint. All the gathered onlookers tut and shake their heads. Friedrich and the man huddle on the floor over Brigitte, pinning her, until two policemen arrive and haul her away.

I look down at my canvas; the wounds are long and threaded, I am cut from boob to belly. A flap of canvas falls forward like a lolling tongue and I wonder if I will ever see the inside of a gallery again.

SLOE WINE

'ROADKILL, EASTER SUNDAY: a badger, a hedgehog, a black cat, a grey cat, a pheasant hen (feathers blowing behind the car), a baby rabbit. Another black cat, two fox cubs, a magpie with a broken tail, a black and white collie.' A pause. 'Probably someone's pet.'

Bernadette heard the snap of the off-button and felt Ralph's self-contained silence sifting like a vapour through the car. The Dictaphone had been her idea: before, Ralph would sit in the back scribbling his lists of roadkill—and other sights of interest—onto a notepad. It was easier to mouth them into the recorder and, like most boys, he enjoyed owning a new gadget.

'All right, pet?' Bernadette said, and Ralph held his mother's gaze in the rear-view mirror and nodded. She had invited him to sit in the front of the car when he had turned twelve, but he preferred the privacy of the back seat. He had space there to store his card games, sketchpads, magazines and MP3 player, and to stretch his ever-lengthening legs. 'Lamb will be happy to see you,' Bernadette said; Ralph didn't answer.

Lamb, her sister Caro's daughter, was thirteen—a year younger than Ralph—and the two cousins had been close up until two years before. Overnight, it seemed, Lamb had moved from tomboy antics to dresses and love songs; she had turned away from Ralph with the casual cruelty of the young. He pretended not to care, but Bernadette knew he found the visits to Callow boring, now that he spent most of his time there alone.

91

Caro was waiting on the avenue for them, a hoe in her hand and a bucket of weeds at her feet. Her skin smelt of leaves when she bent to kiss Bernadette through the rolled-down car window. She said, 'Hi Ralphie', and that lunch was on the table. Bernadette drove up to the house under a canopy of sycamores; since she was a child those trees had reminded her of the thick-branched passageway in *The Sleeping Beauty*. Caro strolled behind the car, still poking at weeds as she walked, swinging her bucket like a handbag.

Lamb was laying the table with plates and glasses when Bernadette and Ralph came into the kitchen; she looked like a youthful version of her aunt crossed with her mother. Her eyes were set too wide like Bernadette's, but she had Caro's fishy pout and shuck of frizz for hair. Lamb hugged Bernadette stiffly and waved a hello at Ralph; he grunted and angled his body away from her. A pile of boiled eggs—decorated with poster paints—sat in a dish in the centre of the table, and there were cling-filmed plates of ham, butterhead lettuce and brown bread.

'We took out last year's sloe wine,' Lamb said, holding up a demijohn; she pulled her lips behind her teeth and frowned.

'I'll have a glass,' Bernadette said, smiling at her niece. 'Should we decant it?'

Lamb popped the bung from the bottle. 'Mam's been pouring it straight from the demi.' She poured a glass for Bernadette, who held it up to look through its ruby core.

'The colour's great. What's it taste like?'

Lamb smiled. 'Not bitter, not sweet. Perfect.'

Every autumn, Lamb and Bernadette picked the sloes from the blackthorn thicket that fenced the bottom of the land; the fruit were always fat. The sloe harvest was a job that Caro hated, but Bernadette was happy to do—her annual nod to childhood activities. Now, at Easter, the blackthorns were heavy with white blossoms; the first sloes wouldn't appear for months.

'Lamb! What do you think you're doing?' The three of them turned to see Caro standing in the back doorway, her hair an angelic fuzz around her face. 'It's barely two o'clock. Do not drink that wine.' Lamb lifted her glass to her lips and drained it. 'You little bitch,' Caro said, lunging at Lamb, who skipped past her and stood behind Ralph, smirking. Caro turned to face Bernadette, her eyes liquid with tears; she shook her head.

'Caro?' Bernadette reached out her hand to her sister but she waved it away.

'I'm fine,' she said, pushing at the tears with her fingers and wiping a streel of muck across her cheek as she did it. Bernadette wet a tea towel at the sink and dabbed it away. 'I'm sorry, Ber. Sorry, Ralph,' Caro said, sitting at the table. She put her forehead onto the tablecloth and started to sob. Bernadette shooed Lamb and Ralph out the back door and sat beside Caro, petting down her hair with one hand.

'Talk,' Bernadette said.

Caro didn't lift her head from the table. 'Mike's back,' she said.

Lamb and Bernadette were standing on ladders, filling plastic buckets with blue-black sloes; the berries' bloomed skins made them look like tiny, frostbitten plums. They could hear each other snuffling from the cold and, every so often, one of them would say something about the thorns or the miserable weather. Their hands were scratched and the rain was starting again; it was near the end of the day and they were sick of running back up to the house during the longer showers. Bernadette lifted her face to the rain.

'Let's keep going—we're nearly done,' she said.

'OK.' Lamb shifted her weight from one bent knee to the other. 'Hey, Ber, what kind of clothes did you and Mam have when *you* were twelve?'

Bernadette looked over to where Lamb was balanced on the stepladder, in her black rubber boots, yellow raincoat and matching hat.

'Pretty much what you're wearing now,' she said.

Lamb sighed. 'Not for working, Bernadette, for ordinary. *God!*'

'Oh, we were scruffy most of the time. Granny made all our clothes—we never had fashions, unless they got passed on from the cousins in America.'

'What did they send?' Lamb threw a handful of sloes into her bucket.

'Nice things: bright T-shirts, short skirts. We both got maxis once—they were lovely.'

'Maxis?'

'Ankle-length dresses—the opposite of minis. They had big flowers all over them.'

'Cool.' Lamb pushed her hand into the mound of fruit she had picked. 'Did you have boyfriends?'

'Not many.'

'What was Mam like back then?'

'Caro? She was a tearaway.' Bernadette smiled. 'Ah no, she was like she is now—her own person—but wilder.'

'How?'

'She was up for anything, any kind of mischief.'

'Like what?' Lamb's face was pinced as she studied her aunt.

'She took part in things: games, adventures. Everyone loved her—boys *and* girls.'

'And what about you, Auntie Ber—were you up for anything?'

'Me? No, I was what was called a square. And what you would probably call a geek.'

'Like me,' Lamb said.

'Honey, you're far from a geek. You're too feisty for that and you're *far* too pretty. No, you're a lot like your Mam.' Bernadette looked up into the blackthorn; there were still plenty of clusters of fruit on the higher branches, but her body was tired and she was hungry. 'All done?' she asked, and Lamb said that she was. They climbed down off the stepladders and lifted the buckets.

'What was my father like?' Lamb said.

Bernadette winced. 'Oh, he was ... handsome.' She heaved her bucket up and looked at her niece. 'We've got a good haul here—enough to make a nice batch of wine.' Lamb nodded and they trudged through the soaking field to the house.

❧

Ralph sat on the back lawn and watched a hare skitter in front of him; it was a small buck and its russet coat shone. The hare stopped, nosed for food, sat up, then ran on and sprang over the dry-stone wall; the lichen on the wall's stones reminded Ralph of bleach splashes. He clicked the record button on his Dictaphone.

'Animals at Callow, Easter Sunday: sheep, calves. A hare —young and very fast.'

'What's that?' Lamb flumped beside him and sprawled out on the grass; Ralph held up the Dictaphone for her to see. She plucked at daisies with her fingers; Ralph looked at her sideways.

'Why'd you drink the wine?' he said.

Lamb shrugged. 'Mam lets me have wine all the time; she just has to show off in front of you and Bernadette. "Look what a *good* mother I am. See how I *care* about my daughter." Huh.'

'Why's she crying?'

'How the fuck would I know?'

'Relax—I don't even care.' Ralph stood up.

'Want to go down to the swimming hole?' Lamb said, getting up too. 'It looks like lunch might be a while. They're still yakking.'

'OK.'

The swimming hole was a murky pond at the far edge of the land. Lamb and Ralph used to swim there, and dip with nets for tadpoles and minnows, when they were younger. They kicked through weeds and stood at the side of the pond, looking at the water grasses and blanket weed that clogged it. Lamb plopped some stones into the green scurf on the water's surface and swung on her heels.

'My father is back,' she said. 'Apparently.'

'Have you ever met him?' Ralph squinted at her.

'No. And I don't want to either.' Lamb shrugged her arms out of her cardigan and threw it on the ground. 'What's the bet he's the reason Mam's crying?' Ralph looked at the spatter of freckles on her wrist and the sleeve-shaped band of white on her upper-arm. It reminded him of fresh things—milk, body lotion, cream. He reddened and turned away. 'Fancy a swim?' Lamb kicked off her runners.

'There's not enough water,' Ralph said. Lamb pulled her T-shirt over her head; she was wearing a swim suit with a low-scooped neck. Ralph looked at the moles punctuating the honeyed skin of her back—they were the same as his own. 'You're mad,' he said, as she waded through the tangle of plants at the water's edge. Lamb turned around; a film of algae clung to her thighs. She splashed water onto her chest, darkening the pink swimsuit.

'Ralphie! Lamb!'

'That's my Mam calling us,' Ralph said.

'*Raaaaalph!* Lunch is ready!'

'Are you coming?'

He looked at Lamb, standing in the middle of the pond. She held his gaze, then unpeeled the top of her swim suit, baring the buds of her chest. Her skin glinted with droplets and she stayed, thigh deep in the muddy water, holding the straps of the suit away from her body, staring at him. Ralph stood on the bank, looking at her small breasts and at her skin, until his mother's shout came again, closer now. He turned away and ran back to the house.

❧

Bernadette had heard Caro leave hours before; now she was back, sliding under her quilt and groaning like a satisfied pup.

'Ber, are you awake?'

'No.'

'Guess where I was?' Caro giggled.

'Shut up and go asleep; I have to be in school early tomorrow.'

'I was with Mike Derridge. And we *did* it.'

Bernadette shoved her head into the pillow and pulled her lips into a knot. 'What was it like?'

'It wasn't *like* anything.' Caro tutted. 'It did hurt a bit though. God, he's gorgeous.'

'Since when have you liked Mike?'

'I dunno. You were going on about him, so I thought I'd check him out.' Caro giggled again. 'And you were right — he's something else.'

The air in the bedroom felt tight around Bernadette's

mouth; she sat up and breathed deep. She looked over to Caro's side of the room and could just make out the navy bulk of her bed.

'Are you his girlfriend now?' Bernadette said.

'I suppose. Good night,' Caro mumbled. Bernadette lay down and turned her back to her sister.

Mike was often at Callow after that. The girls' parents liked him; he was sporty, polite—a good boy. Still, he and Caro weren't to be alone together in the house and Mike was not allowed upstairs. Bernadette was forced into their company and she got used to their touching and kissing while the three of them watched TV. Mike would look at Bernadette over Caro's shoulder as they lay on the sofa holding each other. He would smile or wink. Bernadette knew he only did it to make her blush; she felt triumphant when the heat stayed out of her cheeks and she could stare straight back at him.

இ

Bernadette stood at the kitchen counter, bottling the sloe wine, pouring it carefully through a funnel, then corking the bottles.

'I don't know why you're bothering,' Caro said, from her armchair.

'We can keep a track on how much we're drinking this way,' Bernadette said, scribbling the date on a label. Caro looked over at her sister; Bernadette continued labelling. Caro suddenly bashed the arm of her chair with the book she was reading and Bernadette raised her head.

'"Keep a track?" Are you trying to say that I'm a lush?' Caro said.

'Oh shut up. You're a selfish cow, Caro; this mood you're in is affecting Lamb. She was a brat at lunch, or did you even notice?' Bernadette tapped the counter with the wine funnel. 'Mike's back in town—big deal. The world can't stop.'

'Ralph's not exactly Mr Happy either.'

Bernadette frowned. 'Caro, Mike's not going to come out here and ask you to marry him, you do know that, don't you?'

'And what the fuck is that supposed to mean?'

'You know what it means: you've been waiting for him. For years. And it's not going to happen.'

'So have you,' Caro said quietly.

'Pardon?' Bernadette felt the rise of a blush.

'You heard.' Caro threw her book to the floor and stood up. 'I know all about you two. I've always known, so before you come across all holier-than-thou, remember that.'

'I don't know what you're on about, I—'

Caro came over and grabbed Bernadette's arm. 'Shut up, Ber, just shut up.' She brought her face close. 'You think I haven't a clue, don't you? Well, I'm not stupid,' she said. 'I know that Lamb and Ralph are more than cousins; I've always known.' She pinched Bernadette's arm. 'But that doesn't stop me wanting Mike.'

❧

Mike's racer was parked against the back wall when Bernadette turned into the laneway; her heart popped when she saw it, then settled. He strolled out from behind the shed, puffing on a cigarette.

'I didn't know you smoked,' Bernadette said, hitching her schoolbag to her other shoulder.

'There's a lot you don't know about me.' He hung his head and looked out from under a flop of fringe; Ralph would do the same thing, years later. 'So, how are you, little Bernie?' he said, flicking the butt to the ground.

'Nobody calls me that.' Bernadette walked past him to the house. 'Caro's at her dance class,' she said, though she knew that he knew that already.

'I'm here to see you,' Mike said.

He came close to her and she could smell the bitterness of his breath; she wondered what he'd taste like. Mike put his arms around her and brought his mouth down on hers. The only other boy she'd kissed had filled her mouth with his tongue; Mike didn't. His lips were thick and soft. Bernadette flicked her tongue-tip against his, enjoying the tang of tobacco and the pressure of his hands on her back. She pulled away, took his hand and led him into the house and up the stairs.

The next day her mother asked her if her period had come early; Bernadette shook her head, thinking of the brown-red stain she had lain on all night.

*

Lamb plunked a bag of clanking bottles to the ground and let her legs dangle over the incline into the pond; she handed a wine bottle to Ralph.

'Jesus, I never heard them fighting like that before, did you?'

'No,' he said, pulling at the cork with his teeth. It came out with a deep parp, like a stone landing at the bottom of a well. He took a swig and handed the bottle back to Lamb; she glugged the wine from the neck, gasping for breath between swallows. Some of it dribbled out of her mouth and she laughed.

'It's not bad, is it? Maybe I'll go into full-time wine

making when I get out of here. "Lamb Derridge: Master Vintner". Is that right—vintner? Can a woman be called a master?'

'How would I know?' Ralph said, looking at the dark wine spots around her lips.

'You don't know much, do you?' Lamb said, and Ralph shrugged. 'Do you know who your father is?' Ralph shook his head. 'Well I do. Just found out. Will I tell you?' He didn't answer. 'Give me your tape machine.' Ralph took the Dictaphone from his jeans pocket and handed it to her. Lamb pushed the wine bottle into the muck, hopped up and ran over to the blackthorn bushes; Ralph saw her fiddle with the buttons and bend her mouth to the speaker. He watched her wade back through the weeds. She sat down close beside him and tossed the Dictaphone into his lap. 'His name is on there. You can listen to it or tape over it. Whatever you want.'

Ralph picked up the Dictaphone and shoved it into his pocket. He took a long drink of wine and gargled it in his throat before swallowing; his head felt swimmy. He smiled at Lamb and pressed her nose with one finger. She puckered her mouth and eyed him. Ralph closed his eyes and kissed her hard; she let him probe her lips, then she kissed him back. They pulled apart and looked at each other.

'That's weirder than you think,' Lamb said, and she leaned against Ralph's side. He slid his arm around her shoulder. They sat on, looking down at the choked swimming hole. The air smelt of mud and dewy grass, and their tongues tasted of sloe wine.

MADEMOISELLE O'MURPHY

You died today. I've sat at my window all morning, staring at the untrustworthy spring sunshine hovering over the boulevard, wondering who you thought of in the end. Old Pompadour? Your Polish wife, perhaps? Or me? And I've wondered, too, whether men hold memories like women do, as full-flowering scenes with smells, skin-touches, falling light. But, no. A man's memories are more likely to hang like meat in aspic, still and jellied, trapped in time.

Mon petit roi. What did you remember of me? We were once Louis and Louisa; *'Lou aime Lou'*, you'd whisper, close into the shell of my ear, when you slid over me. *Lou aime Lou aime Lou.* When we were apart, you said, you never spoke of me as a courtesan. You preferred a bawdier line of talk. If you spoke of me at all, it was as queen of your bed in the Parc-aux-Cerfs; I was your cat, your trollop, your blowsy harlot. I was *'la petite Morfi'*, your little Dublin brasser. And while I lived a lady's life in the grounds of the *chateau*, my Ma herded my sisters to the artists' *ateliers* in Montparnasse, hoping for luck like mine for them. And my Da cobbled soldiers' boots down a back lane in Versailles, as he once had on Parliament Street, not a dog's roar from the murky Liffey.

I am always impatient for the next thing: the anticipated outing or a party somewhere new. When stopped in one spot, I choke with impatience. But, there are times when I want nothing to change. So it was with you, Louis, and so it was in Monsieur Boucher's *atelier*. Though, later, I hated Boucher for befriending Madame de Pompadour, when I first met him, as a budding girl, I was content. Oh, they all whispered that Boucher was amoral because his paintings brimmed with passion, but he was a good man. He was like a second father to me and, of course, it was through him that I came to know you.

⁊⁊

Monsieur Boucher wears a green banyan; his toes scallop from the bottom of the robe and they are long, like a monkey's. This makes me giggle. My Ma stops in the doorway when she sees him, then pushes me forward. She is trying to swallow a comment about his dress; I can feel it gagging in her throat.

She squeaks, 'My Louisa, Monsieur.'

'Ah, Mademoiselle O'Murphy.' Boucher bows.

'Isn't she gorgeous, Monsieur? Just like I told ya; a proper Irish colleen.'

The *atelier* smells of rotten fruit, damp clothing and linseed; on an easel there is a portrait of a mutton-as-lamb matron. I wonder if Boucher is mocking the woman by putting that crinkled face on a young body. My Ma blinks at the painting and pushes me toward the artist again; we stare at each other.

'Apple fresh,' Boucher says. He palms money to my Ma and she leaves.

'This place stinks,' I say, and he laughs, his avuncular face creasing. And that was when you came in, *mon roi*, and saw me.

I like to pose—it makes my skin tighten and tingle, and between my thighs grows lax. I was hoping to be painted reclining on my back, so that my breasts could be admired. They are good breasts—round and heavy as grapefruits—

but Boucher prefers me on my front, with my buttocks risen, afloat on a pile of oyster and pink velvet. It is my idea, though, that I should turn my face away from the viewer, as if unaware of being watched.

Boucher allows me to see the portrait as it grows; I slip from the *chaise longue* and we stand by the easel, looking at the portrait. There is no nod to history in it: I am not Diana the Huntress, nor am I a biblical Susannah. This work is neither a commission nor a titillation; it is just me, a girl, lying on her soft belly, in a painting.

'Why the pink rose?' I ask.

Boucher laughs. 'Because you exist somewhere between red and white, Louisa.'

'My right shoulder sits too high and my front knee too low,' I say, and Boucher nods. 'Still, the whole effect is pleasing. The blue ribbon in my hair draws the eye.'

'A clever assessment, Louisa,' he says, touching my bare back with his fingertips.

❧

Did you remember before you passed, *mon roi*, how I styled myself the hungriest harlot? The most daring, the lustiest, the most compliant? You loved me for it. But I was only ever a distraction, was I not? I was too childish to understand what was important to a man outside of bed-lust: peace and war, roads and ships, his wife and children. And, of course, the love and opinions of Pompadour, the queenliest concubine of all. My wants and woes were small by comparison.

I could never think of Pompadour as someone with slippery places, who whispered as she welcomed you inside her; she was too cold-faced. Anyway, I didn't like to think of you in that way with any of the others. But, my musings had their own will and, to comfort myself, I often imagined old Pompadour in her pelt, furred with fine hairs, like a goat, and her nipples—twinned, long purple teats—sticking out from the down. It pleased me to style her as an animal. But my mind conjured an uglier picture: you lying over her, her silly puffed-up hair jiggling as you rocked, back and forth. Then worse: Pompadour straddling you— as you made me do—her face crooked with lust, yours crooked with love. I scribbled those images away and vowed to make you love me the most, for all time.

🙙

My hair smells yeasty after our loving; you cradle your hand over the taut curve of my belly. I have been crying and my eyes are swollen, like a frog's.

'What is it you want, Lou?' you ask. You pull away.

'I want to be treated better,' I pout. 'I want rooms in the *chateau*. Like Madame de Pompadour has.'

You laugh. 'Louisa, you are a child.'

'A child who is with child.' I place your hand on my stomach.

'I would lose all respect.'

'But what of your son or daughter, *mon roi*? What of me?' I caress the pouches of your chest and you purr. Then you throw my hand off.

'I have children enough, Louisa.'

You rise and struggle into your clothes; I lift my cheek for a kiss but you leave the chamber. I lie back against the pillows and survey my body: my nipples are plum-dark and fine hair is growing over my stomach, like vetch on a hillock.

105

NUDE

Madame de Pompadour stands in my room in the Parc-aux-Cerfs. My clothes lie on the floor like a pile of sloughed skins; I would not let the housemaid assist me to undress — the girl pinches me. And she complained when I vomited on the bedroom floor morning after morning.

'Can I help you, Madame?'

Pompadour looks at the skirts and petticoats on the mat, and at my unwound hair. She is tall, slim-waisted, a neatly packaged person. I try to imagine goat hide prickling under her gown, but my mind blurs — her beauty is too present.

'Do you know what my pet name was, as a girl?' she says; I shake my head. 'It was "Reinette". Think about that, Louisa. I was the "little queen".' She glances at me. 'Our dear Louis has been king since he was five years old and, from a child, I was destined to be his greatest love — my mother was told it by a fortune teller. I couldn't marry him, no, but I mean everything to him.' She kicks at my clothes. 'You mean nothing.'

'I am the mother of his child.'

She laughs; a short, deep laugh that does not suit her. 'A bastard daughter. What use is that to a king?'

'At least I am not barren.' I flick my eyes up, sure she will come and hit me. She pulls her mouth up at the corners, faking a smile.

'Murder is very near the surface, Mademoiselle O'Murphy.'

'Is that a threat, Madame?' The words topple out. Pompadour steps towards me, goes to speak, then sighs.

'You will not oust me, Louisa. Whatever you may think.' She points at the floor. 'Tidy your room.'

MADEMSOISELLE O'MURPHY

&

I made a mistake, Louis. Love made me brash and I made a mistake. Perhaps I was too young to be who you made me be. If I was sixteen when you first took me from Boucher's studio, or seventeen, maybe then I would have known I had to keep my counsel to keep my king. But I was a girl. And you evicted me and our child without a thought.

Now you are gone, *mon roi*, and I am an old woman. But still I crave you, as I always have, and I choke with my customary impatience for—at last—I am ready to die.

AMAZING GRACE

EARLY MCINTYRE HAD a badger-stripe of silver flashing through her hair from root to tip. My mother said she should dye it black, to give herself a more youthful appearance. She only said that to us, though, not to Early herself. They had been at school together but were never friends. My mother told us that people said old Mr McIntyre had built a circular house—a place without angles—so that the Devil couldn't lurk in the corners and tempt his daughter.

'The Devil can hide as easily in the human heart as in a corner,' my father said.

My mother humphed. 'Shut bloody up. What do *you* know about the human heart?'

My father shrugged and disappeared back into watching the television.

'Early McIntyre looks like a witch,' my brother Ian said.

'Turn your gossipy mind to higher things, Ian, and stop making assumptions,' I said.

He kicked the leg of my chair. 'Get a life, Grace. You're a gock.'

She had left our village before I was born but, when old Mr McIntyre died, Early turned up and moved back into her childhood home. When I saw her, my skin spurred with excitement. Early was scarily magnificent: she had a silent face, waist-length hair, and a black bike that she teetered around on. Anytime I saw her in the greengrocer's or Horgan's bakery, I took in all about her. I was fascinated by the poppy seed loaves and garlic bulbs she bought, as much as

108

by her flowing clothes, and the head-up way she carried herself. I was sure she never saw me—a gangly eejit with frizzy hair—hovering about. And what I wanted most in those weeks was for Early McIntyre to notice me.

My fourteenth birthday came that August. We had a sponge cake for tea. Ian crowed, 'You look like a monkey and you are one too', when they sang Happy Birthday. I spent those end-of-summer days on the tyre swing in our garden, holding my face up to the clouds. I squinted through the tree branches, imagining a far-off version of myself, where I was comfortable in my own skin and famous for doing something-or-other. It made my gut warm. When I wasn't dreaming on the swing, I cycled in front of the round, limed house on the rise, hoping to find Early on her way in or out.

The road cleaved, poker-straight, from the McIntyre house to the church at the bottom of the village. I would cruise down to the church gates on my bike and pump back up the hill, my thighs screaming, trying to look like I was just passing by. Early never seemed to be around and I thought that she must have gone away again. One afternoon, I lifted the gate latch and walked up to her front window. As I hooshed myself forward to look inside, the window opened and Early's face loomed in front of mine.

'Can I help you?' she whispered, her nose almost touching mine. I jumped.

'Oh, I . . . I was looking . . .'

'Would you like to step inside?' I wasn't sure if it was an invitation or a summons.

'Yes. Please.'

She opened the front door; the whole of the downstairs was one circular, many-windowed room. I smelt a peppery smell, like orchids; it was overlaid with the warm musk of spices. Early took my sweaty hand between her large fingers.

'You're welcome here,' she said. 'I've seen you about.'

I nodded, feeling suddenly small and protected. Up close, I saw that Early's face was raddled but fresh; her cheeks were as firm-looking as unripe tomatoes. She had a caramel tan and moved her voluptuous, animal body easily; she was prettier than she had seemed at a distance.

'What's your name?' she said.

'Grace.'

'Ah, a beautiful name. One to live up to. I'm Early McIntyre.' Her voice came slow, like warm honey.

'I know.'

She pointed to a sofa and I sat. The room was marked out into territories: the kitchen had units curved to fit the walls; the dining room was bright with roadkill-red wallpaper; her sitting room took up the central floor space. A scatter of marble elephants pointed their up-turned trunks at the door and a huge, age-pocked mirror stood against one wall.

'I like to collect things,' Early said, handing me a mug of tea. 'What do you like to do, Grace?'

My tongue felt tangled; I couldn't think of one thing that sounded interesting enough to say to her.

'I love my bike,' I said, eventually. 'Cycling.'

'We'll have to take a bicycle ride together sometime soon, while this warm weather lasts.'

'Cool.'

My mother prepared the picnic; she seemed to want to impress Early.

'Early's been around,' she said. 'Been all over, I mean. What sort of food does she have in that house of hers?'

'Spicy food, curries, that sort of thing. But, you know, a few sandwiches will do fine.'

'Sandwiches? Have a bit of imagination, Gracie, for pity's sake.' My mother hung in front of the fridge, frowning.

I left the house the next morning, lugging enough food, it seemed to me, for seven people. My mother shouted after me that I was to send her best regards to *Miz* McIntyre. Ian shadowed her in the doorway, sniggering. Wishing they'd go back inside, I heaved the food bag into the basket on my bike. It was one of those fresh, not-too-sunny days. We took the main road out of the village; the ditches overflowed with montbretia and red haws. Cycling side-by-side along Icehouse Lane, Early told me she used to play there as a girl with the green slabs of ice. She told me things and asked my opinion, as if what I thought mattered. I watched Early cycle ahead of me, her hair a winding helix down her back, her bum cushioning both sides of the saddle like an over-stuffed pillow. She kept herself erect and sang strings of tuneless gobbledy-gook; it was hard to believe she was the same age as my mother.

We stopped under a sycamore; I was sweaty all over and threw myself onto the blanket that Early spread out. She lay beside me and I listened to our breathing become less of a fight.

'Gorgeous,' Early said.

'What is?' I propped on one elbow to look at her.

'This. Here. Home. The air is so clear, so breathable.' She flicked a daddy-long-legs from her nose. 'India was smothering at times.'

'What were you doing there?'

'This and that. Travelling. Working mostly.'

'Did you like it?' I looked at the band of silver that flowed from her crown through her thick plait. She sat up.

'Yes. The people are warm, inquisitive, generous. Despite their poverty. The women are kept down, though, even the wealthier ones.' Early frowned. 'My friend Sabitha, who was married to a politician, didn't wear lipstick because her husband didn't like it.' She shrugged and started to unpack the picnic. 'Do you plan to travel, Grace?' I had never thought about it but, wanting to please her, I said that I did. 'Travel broadens the heart as much as the mind. It should be *de rigueur* for every young person.'

Early opened the food packets delicately and made a mini buffet. We ate my mother's egg and parsley rolls, heavy slices of date loaf, mandarin oranges; we drank apple juice from cartons. Early consumed everything robustly and said to thank my mother very much. We shared dark chocolate that she broke into pieces and handed to me on a silver dish; she sucked on the chocolate, letting it brown her lips. Swinging two wet-beaded bottles from her bag, she snapped off the caps with her fingers.

'Kingfisher beer. It's Indian.' She handed a bottle to me. '*Most thrilling chilled!*' she read from the label and laughed.

The hoppy beer warmed my throat; after a few gulps, my stomach felt hot. I grinned at Early and she clinked her bottle to mine and said, 'Chin-chin'. I lay back, puckering my mouth over the neck of the bottle to take awkward swigs. Listening to Early sipping hers, I imagined her mouth wet. She half-sat and leaned over me; I scrunched my eyes to focus on her—she seemed to be swaying.

'I love these little kiss-curls you have, Grace.' She wrapped her finger into the hair over my forehead. 'You look like Goya's *Maja*, lying back like that—the clothed version. Do you know the painting?' I shook my head. 'Goya was Spanish. He painted two portraits of the same girl: in one she's nude; in the other she's dressed. They are absolute masterpieces. The *maja* has tendrils around her face. Like yours.'

I smiled and my eyes fixed on the plumpness of Early's lips; I could smell the sweet fug of her breath and see her small teeth, perfect inside her mouth. Leaning up, I closed my eyes and let my lips touch hers. She darted the tip of her tongue between my teeth, pressed her mouth to mine, then drew away. We stared at each other, then Early lay back and I flumped alongside her.

'Have I told you how I got my name?' she said, after a few minutes.

'No.'

'It's kind of obvious really.' She giggled. 'I was born seven months after my parents' wedding: I was a strapping bouncer—hitting ten pounds.' She paused and my ears filled with countryside sounds: a far-off tractor-whirr, clicking insects, the tussle of leaves. 'My mother insisted that I was premature and, to reinforce the point, she christened me "Early".'

'I love your name.'

'Thank you, Grace.'

She touched my hand; I wound my fingers into hers, listened to the soft buzz of insects and closed my eyes. I fell into a light sleep, still holding her hand in mine.

My parents huddled on the end of my bed; my mother poked my father, trying to get him to speak but all that came out of his mouth were small grunts. I sat with my arms tucked around my knees, staring at my father's nostrils, the bend of his ears. My mother's breasts were low and lumpy under a T-shirt and her mouth was tugged sideways from the constant scowl she wore. I picked sleep grit from my eyes, wanting and not wanting them to get on with what they had come to say.

'What?' I said.

My father fiddled with the eiderdown.

'Well, Grace, the thing is, your mother feels,'—prod-poke with one finger from her—'that is, *we* feel that you're spending too much time with Ms McIntyre. With Early. She's a grown woman and you're probably bothering her. I'm sure she has things to do.' He looked at my mother. '*We're* sure.'

I stuck out my bottom lip, rolled it back and forth—it was something Early did when she was thinking about what she wanted to say next.

'Early likes my company.' I eyeballed them. 'She says that I'm refreshing.'

'Pfffff.' My mother shook her head.

'What?' I said.

'*Refreshing*,' she said.

'And what would you know about it?' I poked her shoulder to emphasise my words: 'You. Stupid. Old. Bag.'

I saw my father's hand and twisted away but his palm slammed into my jaw; I careened backwards, knocking my head off the wall.

'Jesus,' my mother yelped, jumping up. My father's breath puffed through his nose in short spurts, like a horse. I crouched on the bed and they stood for a few moments before backing out of the room.

'It smells like dung.'

I was sitting on Early's sofa; she was holding a poultice to my face: muslin packed with a mish-mash of who-knew-what.

'It smells perfectly fine.'

She lifted it away, looked, winced, then replaced it. My jaw felt puffed out and sore.

'I suppose I look like a toad.'

'Yes, you do, Miss Toad of Toad Hall.'

The length of her thigh was pressed to mine; I looked up at her face, the steep arch of her eyebrows, her thin lashes. She flashed a grin at me.

'Thanks,' I muttered, and she nodded, pouting her lip.

'So, are you going to tell me *why* he hit you?'

'Oh, bless me Father for I have sinned, I called my mother a bad name . . .'

'You didn't, did you?' Early lifted the poultice away. 'I'm surprised, Grace. Why did you do that?'

I pussed, but she urged me on, so I told her they had said I was to keep away from her. Early plopped the sopping muslin into a bowl. She sighed and said maybe they were right; maybe it wasn't OK for us to be together so much.

'What do you mean?'

'You have your school work to think of now, with the new term starting. It's probably time to concentrate on that.'

'But Early, I—'

'No buts, Grace. How can I go against your parents?'

She slid off the sofa and went to the sink. I watched while she cleaned out the bowl with a spray of water: I could see her bra strap through the material of her blouse, the violin-curve of her waist and hips. Going to where she stood, I slid my arms around her from behind.

'Have I ever told you how I got my name?' I whispered into her shoulder, starting to cry. She turned and took me in her arms, wiping at my tears and snots with her sleeve.

'No, you haven't.'

I dropped my head onto her chest and she twisted one

hand through my hair and rubbed the small of my back with the other.

'Ian is six years older than me. My mother always wanted lots of kids so, after him, she kept trying for another baby, but nothing happened. She had tests done but they didn't find anything wrong with her. Three years after having Ian, she got pregnant again and was thrilled. But after four months, she lost the baby. She had three more miscarriages after that, one on top of another. My father didn't want to try any more—my mother was so sad each time another baby didn't live. Her doctor said to stop too.' Early took my hand and led me back to the sofa. 'My mother *knew* she could have a baby, so she just kept on trying. When everyone else had given up, she got pregnant with me. And I stuck.' I squeezed Early's hand. 'If I was a girl and if I lived, my mother swore she'd call me Grace: Latin for 'the loved', 'the favoured', 'the honoured'. So she did.'

'That's a beautiful story,' Early said. 'And I *adore* your name. Grace, the loved. Grace, the favoured. Grace, the honoured.' She bent low, took my face in her hands and kissed my nose. 'Amazing Grace.'

I put my arms around her neck. Early hugged me tight and we held each other, both sobbing, until the round room grew dusk-dark and all I could see were shadows fingering towards the ceiling. I breathed in the smoky smell of her hair and felt the slack heat of her weight against me; my eyes were heavy from crying. When she fell asleep, I pulled myself from her arms and made my way home.

JUNO OUT OF YELLOW

IS IT VAIN TO LOVE a portrait of yourself? My mother didn't think so. *Juno Out of Yellow* hung—and still hangs—in the City Gallery. We used to visit it together. Mother would squeeze Father's arm and say what a great artist he was, and how lovely she herself looked in the painting. Father had wanted to paint her like Botticelli's Venus—powerful and demure—but she argued for a Flemish-type Bathsheba and, as always, he obeyed. He portrayed Mother being helped out of a yellow cloak, her alabaster breasts pouched, her face turned away.

I am in the painting. Or at least my twelve-year-old self is: I'm the girl behind Bathsheba, who pulls the cloak—in real life it was a towel—from her arms. I look attentive, while she is distracted, but we are alike: long noses, dark hair, prim mouths. Like most people, I own a postcard of *Juno Out of Yellow*, but sometimes I love to go to the gallery, to stand in front of it. I enjoy looking at Mother and me as Biblical mistress and maid, and at Father's brushstrokes. He was always lavish with oil; it took months for his paintings to dry. Linseed and turpentine were the scents of my childhood.

❧

Mother sits, shawled in the yellow towel, on the edge of a chair; I'm on the floor. The seat's cane-work has made a criss-cross pattern on her behind; I can see it when she rocks her body, but I don't tell her, in case she gets angry.

My eyes linger on the bush of hair between her thighs, comparing it mentally to my own spare sproutings. She holds up a hand mirror and slicks one finger over each eyebrow. Tilting her chin, she redoes her lipstick.

'I'm fed-up prinking; if I fiddle any more with myself, I'll look like a fucking corner girl. Can we get on with it?'

'No cursing in front of Isabelle, Juno.'

'Oh, fuck off, Desmond.'

Father crosses his eyes at me and I smile. Then I glance at Mother; she doesn't like being left out.

'Fix Izzy's hair,' he says.

Mother pulls me between her legs and pinces me with her knees. Her smell is sweet-sharp, like buttermilk. She flicks through the ends of my hair with a brush, then pulls it from the crown in even strokes; the sound fills my ears with a comforting thrum-thrum-thrum.

'Your turn now,' I say, hopping up. I start on her hair; the tines snag and she jerks.

'Go easy!'

I run the hairbrush gently over the smoothening strands. Mother purrs and wiggles her neck. I look at her nipples pointing from under the towel like two plum-coloured hazelnuts.

'Thomas is visiting us today,' she says.

'Thomas?' says Father, as if he doesn't know who she's talking about. He continues to mix paints, his face creased.

'Yes, Desmond. *Thomas*.' Mother snaps the brush from my hand and gets up.

'Is he visiting us, or visiting you?' Father asks.

'Where do you want Isabelle to stand?' Mother shucks the towel from her shoulders.

'Does he have to come today? I wanted to really *start* on the painting.'

118

'Will here do?' Mother pushes me behind her and faces him.

'Yes, Juno. There will do.'

Father asks Thomas to wait in the parlour.

'I'd like to stay and watch, if it's all the same to you,' Thomas says, smiling, 'see the master at work.'

He perches on Father's paint-mixing table and tips cigarette ash into a jam jar. I can't see Mother's face, but the air has shifted around us. I lift my eyes. Thomas has sideburns; he is jauntily handsome, like a film star. I want him to look at me and I wish that I was naked too. He pouts a small kiss across to Mother, catches me watching, and winks.

'Can we have wine, Desmond?' Mother asks.

'Isabelle. Eyes down, please,' Father says.

'Red or white, Thomas?' Mother says.

'Mmm, red for me.'

'I want to do another hour or two.' Father stands with his palette tucked in front of him, like a shield.

'We have tomorrow,' Mother says. 'And the day after that. And the day after that.' She giggles. 'How often do we have guests?'

'Isabelle, get your mother her robe,' Father says.

Mother is tucked on the couch in her silk robe, with Thomas at her feet; they drink wine until their teeth are grey.

'Don't you have something to do, Isabelle, other than hover?' Thomas says.

'Oh, shut up, Tommy; she's excited by visitors, stuck out here in the back-arse of nowhere. Aren't you, Izzy?'

'It depends on the visitor,' I say.

Mother hoots. 'Isn't she a scream? *So* serious. Just like Desmond.'

Thomas stares at my face. 'Be a good girl and get more wine for Juno and me.'

I glance at Mother and she nods.

The kitchen is dark, though light spills across from the studio. I make two cheddar sandwiches; Father and I eat them in silence, looking at the painting.

'It's going to be special,' I say.

'Yes, my love. It is.'

I stand in the doorway. Mother's robe is peeled back and Thomas is leaning onto her, cradling her breasts with his long hands and sucking at her neck. She grunts and I can hear the sloppy noise of his mouth on her skin. He must be squashing her, I think.

'Here's your wine.'

Mother slides out of view below the couch and Thomas plunks himself into a sitting position.

'You shouldn't sneak up on people,' he says.

'I thought you were gone to bed, Izzy.' Mother's lipstick is fuzzed around her mouth.

'Father is still in the studio,' I say, and leave.

§•

Look closely at *Juno Out of Yellow*. Lift your eyes past the nude figure and the clothed one; past the folds of the cloak and the heavy blue walls. Most people haven't realised that there is a third person in the painting. In the mirror, behind Mother and me, you will see a face—a Le Brocquyian ghost of whites, with two slashes of black;

nicotine-brown smoke rises above this figure, whose mouth is a stretched leer.

I didn't see Thomas again after the night with the wine, and Mother and Father never mentioned him.

IN SEED TIME, LEARN

THE LIGHT BULB over the table burst and the kitchen went dark; bits of bulb glass landed in my hair and I shook my head and swiped them away.

'Shit,' Imogen said, reaching across to touch my arm, 'it must be a power surge.'

'It's Dana,' I said, standing up, 'she's dead.'

'For fuck's sake, Sonny. What are you talking about?' Imogen snapped her hand away and fumbled towards the hall. 'This one's gone too,' she shouted. I heard her bump into the coat stand and curse, then head up the stairs to the nursery.

I knew Dana was dead, as surely as I knew anything. And although I had weaned myself off the idea of her—of us— I felt panicked at the thought of never seeing her again. I sat down, my mind pulling backwards to Dana and our pact: when one of us died, we had said, the light bulbs in the other's house would blow. All of them, spectacularly. We had made this deal as twelve-year-olds, cooped in the hut we had built in her garden, high on each other's salt and clay smell, our mouths raw from a long 'session'.

'Are you up for a session?' Dana would say, standing at my parents' hall door; I would nod and follow her to the hut. There we would huddle and kiss, locking lips and licking the insides of each others mouths, stopping and starting to perfect some flick or linger of the tongue. Dana made it clear, after each session, that we were not boyfriend-girlfriend.

'It's practice,' she would say, 'for when we meet someone to love.'

Dana was an adult-in-waiting, impatient to slough off
her child's skin and become a real person; I followed
behind.

But I don't want to get quagmired in childhood memories; whole seasons and geographies are rearranged in my
head, with the truth a wispish version of itself. Now she is
dead and I would rather talk about Dana as I knew her last;
the Dana who became my lover.

I hadn't been on a plane in a while—Imogen has never
liked to fly—and I felt foolishly important and pleased
with myself. I chose a window seat, so I could watch the
take-off. Nobody sat beside me and I was enjoying the wonder of the views from the window: sheep like grains of rice
scattered on fields; a lumpy swathe of sea pocked with fer-
ries; the contrail of another plane morphing from a thin to
a puffed out line. My mind was mulling these things—as
well as the research I was on my way to France for—when
I felt a hand on my knee. Forgetting Imogen was back at
home, I cupped my hand over it and squeezed. Then, as if I
had been bitten, I snatched my hand back and turned sideways; Dana was grinning at me, her pinch-pale face barely
changed in twenty-five years.

'Hello, Sonny,' she said.

'Dana, my God. Wow.' I hugged her, breathing her earth
and sweat scent, doused now in perfume. 'How are you?
You're here.'

'Yes, I'm here. And I'm grand. Grand.' She pulled her
hands over her dark Joan of Arc hair, tamping it down. 'So,
Paris?'

'Yes, for a week. I'm researching the origins of Irish apples, for a radio show.' I smiled at her. 'You should hear the names, they're gorgeous.' I told her about the Orléans Reinette, the queen of sweet, dry apples; about the Bloody Butcher and the heart-shaped Cavan Strawberry. 'There's even one with my name,' I said.

'The "Sonny"?'

'No, the "Valentine".'

'What's that one like, tasty?' She smiled and I thought how great she looked—a child stretched out into a perfect adult.

'The Valentine's a little dry. Large too, and a bit uneven.'

'Very apt.'

We both laughed; I felt my face redden and looked away.

'Sorry, I'm waffling,' I said. 'What will you get up to in Paris?'

'Not much. Sleeping, eating, drinking. Walking.'

'We should get together.'

'Yeah, Sonny, I'd like that,' Dana said.

I studied her face, trying to gauge if she meant what she'd said; midlife paranoia had started to creep in and I second-guessed everyone. I was really hoping we would meet.

We had tarte Tatin for dessert in Le Grenier de Notre Dame; the pastry was burnt underneath but the tier of apple slices was sour-sweet and delicious. I picked at some toasted almonds and watched Dana suck slivers of caramelised fruit off her spoon; I was surprised at how well I remembered her lip-shape: thin, with an appealing red bump at the bow.

She had taken my hand when I met her in the foyer of her hotel; she held it all the way down Boulevard Saint

Michel, on our way to the restaurant, and I left it there, not knowing what else to do. Her gloves were crimson leather, mine were black; I thought, incongruously, of the wolf leading Red Riding Hood into the wood.

'Cold,' I said.

'But not raining.' Dana squeezed my hand.

There was a mix of the familiar and the new in being around her and I had a giddiness in my chest that I hadn't felt in years. I was skittish, chatty, wanting to discuss things that were about us, and only us. Wine often made me like that—gregarious and life-loving—but I recognised that there was something else here; something that I was playing for and that I wanted.

'Do you remember our "sessions"?' I said, when we had scraped the last of the spicy apple off the pastry and into our mouths.

Dana giggled. 'Of course I do. It was all worth it; people tell me I'm a great kisser.'

I looked at her mouth again. 'Do you want to go for a wander?' I said.

'Sure.'

We linked arms as we headed towards the Seine and the hulk of Notre Dame. Part of me wanted to feel tense—like a betrayer—but it was as if my life with Imogen existed on another plane, and it was impossible then to muster myself as part of it. I liked the weight of Dana's arm on mine, the brush of her coat; I felt I had always been with her, or that I should have been.

We stood in the square in front of the cathedral with all the other tourists, and examined the rows of angels and saints above the doorway. The outdoor Christmas tree— still clinging on, though it was the end of January—swayed and twinkled, its red baubles bouncing on the branches.

'It's incredible,' Dana said, and I pulled her flush to me and closed my mouth over hers. She tasted and felt the same as ever under my tongue, and I suddenly wanted to cry.

Her room was small, like most Parisian hotel rooms, but it was clean, unshabby. I didn't want to bring her to my hotel, it seemed too deliberate. On the short Métro ride to her street, Dana showed me a tiny photo of Marty, her husband, and a ridiculous jealousy winnowed in me.

'What are we doing?' I said, standing at her bedroom window, watching the light beam from the tip of the Eiffel Tower swoop over the roof tops.

Dana came to me and held me from behind. 'Whatever you want.'

'Whatever I want?' I said. 'What about this husband of yours?'

'I'm not some sort of Eve, Sonny, offering you an apple. You have a wife.' Dana let her arms drop from my waist and sat on the bed.

'I'm going to go,' I said.

'Suit yourself. There are no rewards for doing the right thing.' She lay down, her back to me.

The next morning, I took a bus to l'Isle-Adam to meet Monsieur Prudhon of Les Croqueurs de Pommes. The bus made slow progress from Porte-Maillot, across the river and down avenues of schools, office blocks and apartment buildings. I wondered what it would be like to live in Paris, to struggle through the blockades of language and history and custom. I was charmed by the idea of myself living there, but the reality of it also wearied me. Once outside the city, the bus trundled through the uncluttered landscape of another era:

the combed fields were free of pylons and they were edged with stands of slim trees; a lone house appeared every so often, tucked low on the horizon.

I met Prudhon in his office in the town and we talked apples; I scribbled his comments and suggestions for further research into my notebook, then he took me to a street market to try some fruit. While he lifted this apple and that for me to taste, my mind slipped over Dana; I wished I hadn't left her so abruptly the night before.

Dana was outside my hotel when I got back, jumping from toe to toe to get warm; she was wide-eyed, as if she could not quite believe the cold.

'How did the pomology go?' she said.

'Great. Come up?'

She followed me into the miniscule lift and we stood close, front to front, looking over each other's shoulders. In my room, she slid to the floor, her back to the radiator.

'It's fucking freezing.'

'I bought you an apple,' I said, pulling it from a paper bag.

'Oh yeah?' She took it. 'What's this one called?'

'It's called "I'm Sorry, I'm A Big Eejit".'

Dana sniggered. 'Really?'

'Actually, it's called a Bisou Rose: a Pink Kiss.' I sat beside her on the carpet and nudged her with my elbow. 'I'll be the serpent if you'll be Eve.' She grinned, and grabbed the apple.

I kissed Dana through a mouthful of Bisou Rose; she pushed some of it onto my tongue and we munched the fruit and giggled, juice wetting our lips. Lifting her onto my bed, I undressed her and, while I did, she watched my face.

I moved down her body, kissing her throat, her nipples, her breastbone, the small hill of her belly; her skin was as soft as milk and baby-firm. She pushed her head back into the pillow and I looked up at the steeple of her nose, the wide church of her mouth and chin; I slid back up along her body.

We made love slowly and thoroughly, keeping our eyes locked together. It was as if we were tuned to fit and move perfectly; I had never felt as able for sex or as involved. Her arching back and irregular thrusts had me teetering all the time. I came and shuddered, my mouth sucked onto her shoulder; I unbent my arms and lay on top of her.

Dana was morbidly out of breath and she swung suddenly from under me, doubling over and clutching at her chest. Her hands rattled.

'Are you OK? Did I hurt you?' I reached for her.

She batted me away. Her shallow panting echoed a far-off curl-up on the mud floor of our hut. We were chased by her older brothers, through brambles and across streets and, when we got to the hut, Dana collapsed on the floor, shaking. She was often breathless but, that time, I was afraid; her hands jerked and her eyes looked dead. I ran to her house and told her mother, who sent me straight home. In my memory, their family moved to Dublin very soon after that and we didn't see each other anymore.

Dana swivelled on the bed and pushed her hands over her sweating face. 'I have a bockety heart, Sonny. And I've been weaning myself off my tablets.'

'Are you allowed to do that?'

'No.' She pulled deep to find some breath. 'The pills block my adrenaline, but from time to time, I miss it; I want waterfalls of it, so I can feel alive.'

She shivered and I pulled the sheet and blanket over her;

I ran my fingers up through her hair, over her scalp.

'Why are you in Paris on your own, Dana?'

'Same reason you are. Marty hates aeroplanes. Just like your wife.'

I didn't believe her.

We met at Victor Hugo's house on the place des Vosges. I got there first and watched children in the square playing on the see-saw and dashing about on scooters and rollerblades, while their parents hovered. Dana trotted under the stone arcade towards me, looking fragile and robust, as only she could; I wondered if she had ever thought about having kids.

We walked the rooms of the Hugos' apartment, marvelling at the over-the-top wallcoverings and carpets, which all matched in a swirl of brown florals.

'Imagine this in candlelight,' Dana said, 'the absolute gloom.'

'They must have been loaded,' I said, looking at the huge portraits of the writer, his wife and family.

Dana pointed at an etching of a beautiful girl with piled, braided hair. 'I doubt if this one was hung when they lived here. It's Juliette, his mistress. Well, one of them.' We both examined the portrait. 'She was with him for fifty years. Do you think we'll last that long?' I frowned and she laughed. 'The face on you! I'm only joking.'

She walked away, on through the rooms, and I caught up with her beside Hugo's tiny four-poster bed; she kept her eyes forward and I stood behind her in the cramped space by the bed.

'This is a one time thing,' I said. 'There's Imogen.'

'Stop freaking out,' Dana said, 'I'm not in love with you, Sonny.'

I felt flat. We shuffled through the rest of the apartment without comment, leaving to walk under the arcades to rue Saint Antoine; we filed into the first bistro we saw. I ordered coffees and watched the waiters rush and fuss, keeping their hierarchy intact.

'I often think about Marty being unfaithful and leaving me. It's a kind of torture but it keeps up my interest, makes him precious to me.' Dana stirred sugar into her coffee. 'Now here I am with you.' She stared at me. 'Why, I wonder? So he doesn't get in there first? To prove something to myself? Jesus, it's so tired.'

'It doesn't feel tired. I love being with you,' I said.

'But it's a one time thing, right?'

'It has to be, Dana.' I tapped my spoon on my cup. 'Imogen is expecting; she's due in March.'

'Fuck. Why didn't you say something, Sonny? Congratulations.' She pulled her fingers over her hair, making a dark helmet of it. 'Yeah, congrats.'

'Thanks,' I said.

Imogen felt the change in me; I stayed away, working and reworking the radio programme. I was wary of touching her. She complained that I was never home, that she was lonely. I watched her grow as if from a distance, our unborn daughter making a ripe fruit of her small body. We bought a pram and a cot and I told her about Dana.

'Are you in love with her?' Imogen said, her face collapsed.

'What? No. God, no. It was just a thing. Some . . . thing.'

'You didn't have to tell me.'

'I'm sorry. It was making me sick.'

Imogen went to stay with Vanessa, her sister.

The first night she was gone, I called Dana's mobile but

it rang out; I had nothing to say to her anyway. Nothing to offer. Imogen came home after three days. She stood in the doorway of our bedroom, cradling her bump, looking at me as if I was a stranger.

'Vanessa's harder to live with than you,' she said.

'Did you tell her what I did?'

'I wouldn't embarrass myself.'

When Eve was born, we made a pact: we would work harder on being close; we would be a tight family. United. And when I promised that to Imogen—fidelity and unity and strength—I really felt like I meant it. So when Dana died, I didn't go to her funeral, in case Imogen took it as a betrayal. Dana's husband left two messages about the arrangements on my voicemail; he sounded matter-of-fact, impatient, hurried; and he had a French accent. I wasn't expecting that.

ACKNOWLEDGMENTS

Thanks goes to the editors of the following publications where many of these stories first appeared: *The Arabesques Review*, *The Cúirt Annual 2009*, *Crannóg*, *Every Day Fiction*, *The French Literary Review*, *Horizon Review*, *Litro*, *Ropes 2009*, The Stinging Fly's *These Are Our Lives* anthology, *The Stinging Fly*, *Southword* and *Ulster Tatler*.

'Mademoiselle O'Murphy' won the inaugural Jonathan Swift Award; 'Before Losing the Valise, But Mostly After' won The Leyney Writers Award; 'Amazing Grace' was short-listed for the In the Footsteps of Aidan Higgins Prose Competition.

I am grateful to my parents Hugh and Nuala O'Connor, who inspired a passion for art, and to my sister Nessa, who fed that passion with her own art and that of others.

For support, patience, friendship and love, I want to thank Finbar McLoughlin, John Dillon, Órfhlaith Foyle, Ma, Da and all the O'Connors, my sons Cúan and Finn, and my baby daughter Juno. Thanks also to my writing group, The Peers, for being fun and supportive. Big thanks to William Wall and Robert Olen Butler; and to John Berger for permission to use a quote from *Ways of Seeing*. And, of course, heartfelt thanks to the Salt team, most especially Jen Hamilton-Emery, for working on this book with such grace and good humour.